MISHA

LANNING'S LEAP BOOK 1

Kathi S. Barton

WCP

World Castle Publishing, LLC
Pensacola, Florida

Copyright © Kathi S. Barton 2014
Print ISBN: 9781629891385
eBook ISBN: 9781629891392
First Edition World Castle Publishing, LLC, August 15, 2014
http://www.worldcastlepublishing.com

Licensing Notes

Cover: Karen Fuller
Photography: Xie4to-graphy
Editor: Eric Johnston
Editor: Maxine Bringenberg

CHAPTER 1

He thought he'd lost it again. Backtracking to the last point he was sure he'd had it, Misha stood there for several seconds with his nose in the air. He felt his brother, Thomas, touch his mind. Misha spoke before Thomas could.

This is the stupidest tracking I've ever done. Why the hell...? It's been two fucking weeks. How the hell are we supposed to find anything now? Thomas laughed then. *This is so not funny.*

You mean the great and powerful Misha Lanning is stumped? Oh my...shit. I should call the media. Hey, I know, I'll call that cute little newspaper girl. The one that said she'd get lost so you'd find her. What was her name again? You think she'd give you some incentive to find her quicker?

Are you fucking finished? Thomas just laughed harder. *How's your luck in finding the other guy? Or are you too busy busting my chops to be looking very hard? Mother fuck, why are we even here?*

Being a hunter was not all that much fun anymore. And the criminals? They were getting smarter and a good deal more violent. But these men...well, they were about the worst he'd seen. No rhyme or reason to what they were doing, and each death was more brutal than the last.

Misha had come to the conclusion, as had his brothers, that there were two men taking and killing the women. The case had grown cold only in the sense that there were no new leads to ending this spree of killings; they were still killing. Misha and his brothers had only been called in late last night, and after spending ten minutes looking over the police reports, they'd come to realize it was two that they were dealing with, not just a single man.

How do you suppose they didn't realize it wasn't possible for one man to do both crimes on one day? Thomas laughed, but this time it was not filled with humor. *Laziness? Stupidity? By the way, no, I've gotten a couple of scent markers, but nothing I can follow well.*

Shit. And both I would guess on the cops. Have you ever seen a fatter bunch of men in your life? Misha found another scent and took it as deeply into his nose as he could. *I just found something. Let me scout around for a bit.*

Misha started after the smell. His cat snarled at him once when they came across the scent of another male who had pissed against a tree, but he didn't stop. He moved further away from it rather than piss his leopard off more. He'd been pissy enough lately and he didn't want to deal with him again.

He was restless, both he and his cat. Lately it had been harder and harder for both of them to stay focused on any task, no matter the size. And the fact that his brother seemed to be having the same issues didn't help. Maybe they needed to get laid more.

I found something new here. Misha stopped running to hunker down in the grass when Andrew, his other brother, spoke. *It's human, but I think I smell wolf, too. Could be it's not human at all.*

Misha asked if any of the others had run into a wolf. No one had, but that could mean they'd simply missed it due to the age of the scent. He told them to be careful, then heard something just to his left. He froze in mid-step.

In an open field it was hard enough to hide, but the dead of summer just made things impossible. He and his cat stood out like a sore thumb. Being a spotted leopard really hurt them at times like this. Misha slowly lowered his body down into the grass and watched as a man walked nearly atop him.

I have one, he told his brothers. Misha slowed his breathing almost to a stop so as not to bring unwanted attention to himself. *Male, thirty to thirty-five. Dark hair with a sharp cut. About six foot, two hundred thirty or less.* Carter asked him the plan. *Nothing for now. He has a woman, but she's already dead.*

The woman was dead, that much was obvious. Misha couldn't hear anything from her, and if that wasn't enough, her throat was slit, like the others had been, as were both her wrists. She'd be drained, too, he'd bet, just like the last three victims had been. After she was killed and hung to bleed out, she'd be taken somewhere and displayed in a fashion that, frankly, made Misha a little ill.

When he's out of my sight, I'll backtrack and see if I can get something on his mode of transport. The others agreed that would be the best way to do it, but, of course, caution was to be used more than anything. He knew this and had to hold his temper not to snap back that he did.

I'm coming toward you from the road. I'll meet you at the far end of the last lot we passed. Rider, Misha's younger brother by only nineteen months, was a worrier.

Not just a little, either. He was a bigger worrier and pain in the ass than their mom. He cleared his throat as he continued. *Have a care, big brother, you know his kind runs in packs.*

Misha smiled. It was just like Rider to give him advice. And as the oldest, Misha took it with the seriousness that it was given to him. Rider was nothing if not cautious.

Carter, the third oldest, was the perfect middle child...happy, rarely serious, and never still. He was the most difficult to work with lately, too. His ability to get into trouble was famous: or, Misha supposed, infamous.

Thomas was...Thomas. He was serious but not painfully so; organized to the point you wanted to brain him; and would tear you a new ass if you messed with his routine. Misha and the others would go into his room and move things out of their perfect order just to fuck with him. That was until he'd had a lock installed. But they had a plan to get in anyway.

Andrew was the clown of them all. His idea of a good time was running naked across a crowded street, or painting the local cops' cruisers a nice shade of puke green. He'd also been known to drop water balloons off the water tower when people were below him...usually only people who had pissed him off, which wasn't all that easy to do.

Then there was Phillip. *Ah, Phillip*, Misha thought...the youngest, yet he was usually the one they'd go to for advice. It could be about anything, too, including women, which was sad but true. He went out more than all of the rest of them together, and had a way about him with the fairer sex that brought up the jealous streak in them all. He was thoughtful, friendly, and smart, too.

Not that they weren't all smart. Their mother had made sure that they knew three things in addition to having a good education. She would beat those things into their heads daily until it stuck.

One was to know how to treat a woman. No matter what she did to them, women were smaller, usually softer, and rarely big enough to take them on. Misha thought his mom might need to get out more on that one. Women were a great deal stronger and meaner than she'd led them to believe. Also, they needed to take responsibility for their actions, even if they had to sacrifice something they loved in order to fix it. The third—and possibly the most important of them—was that family was all you ever had, so take care to keep them safe and near to your heart.

Where did you go? Rider sounded impatient, and Misha laughed a little. *When you say you're going to be somewhere, you should at least show up.* Misha felt his temper snap in less than a second.

Next time I find a man walking in front of me with a dead woman in his arms that he'd more than likely killed while I was looking for him, I'll make sure to expose myself. That way I can get to you in a timely manner and not fuck up your way of thinking.

I'm sorry. Misha came into the clearing just as Rider apologized to him again. *I was worried about you, and when I didn't see you...well, after last month, I worry more than I should.*

Misha shivered. Last month. Last month he'd nearly been killed, and still had bad dreams about it. Before he could go down that path again, Misha saw Rider drop to the ground suddenly.

A car pulled into the lot beside his brother. Misha dropped down as well but was ready to move if Rider needed him. Neither one moved as the car just sat there with the engine off. Misha made a mental note of the plate number and told Andrew what it was so he could remember as well.

Rider was closer and more than likely had a better sense of what was going on. But Misha moved around the tree line, keeping his brother in sight. When he was within ten yards of him, the car door opened and a man got out. Christ, he was fucking big, but not nearly as big as Misha was. Misha knew that if the guy attacked any of them he could take him, and would if necessary.

Wolf, was all Rider said, and Misha moved faster. When the wolf moved to the other side of the car and opened the door, Misha stilled. If the wolf looked up or caught even a small breeze, he'd know that Misha was there. He was terrified that the man was reaching for a gun. He felt that way nearly every time he was in one of these situations now. Being shot once would do that to you, three times would make you insane with fear of it happening again.

The woman spilled out of the car and only just missed hitting the ground before the wolf caught her with his knee. Even from a distance, Misha knew she was as good as dead. The woman had been worked over badly and her body was barely hanging on. Even if the ambulance was there with them, he doubted it would be soon enough to save her.

Should we follow him? Rescue the girl? What? Misha didn't know and said as much. He explained that the woman was nearly dead. *Well, she's alive now. I can almost bet she won't be if we wait much longer.*

Carter came up beside him and Misha told him what was going on. The woman had been lifted and was now resting on the wolf's shoulder. The scent of the wolf, his excitement over whatever he was doing, seemed to roll off him. Just as Misha had decided to attack, a human seemed to appear out of nowhere. The man carried the same scent Misha had found in the woods.

"I thought you'd have her there by now." The human lifted the woman's head up by her hair and stared at her face for several seconds before dropping her back down again. "She'll have to do."

"You'd think of all the fucking humans around I'd be able to pick one that could survive a few tests, wouldn't you?" Carter looked at Misha when the wolf started bitching. "I mean, it's not like we're asking them to do all that much. Just lay there and let us see how long they can last. Fuck, and this one is heavy."

The last victim they'd recovered had been killed by mutilation, a great deal of it. After the men had cut her belly open, then her thighs, they'd broken both her legs and arms. She'd been hung upside down after she was immobilized, then her throat was cut. She'd bled out while she hung there. But this woman looked—

"So this time you started at the other end of the process?" The wolf nodded to the human as they moved through the dense woods. "I don't think it was any better. In fact, it looks like she lasted less than the others. We need to find a way to make her suffer before she dies. It's what keeps me staying with her, knowing that she's going to suffer."

"You sure we can't just kill her now? The police have given up, yeah, but this is boring now. I want to play with men, too. Fuck them up like they deserve." Misha and Carter followed the men at a safe distance. Rider stayed behind to wait for the other brothers and to have one of them go back the way the other man had come.

"She's a fucking cunt, but Christ, she's driving me over the edge daily. Last night she...."

Misha tuned the human out and spoke to Rider. *Call the police. The woman is dead, but we need to end this. They are far from finished killing, and even if we never find where they were, we at least will have them behind bars.*

I'm sending Andrew and Phillip around in front of them to head you off. Thomas is on his way to find the other woman to see if he can get her before any animals do. He said he lost her scent when the man came around, but he's sure he can find it now. Misha thanked him. *Be careful. I can't...please, just be careful.*

After assuring him that he would, Misha stopped by what appeared to be an abandoned shack. Misha told Andrew and Phillip to come back to it. The reports they'd read had never mentioned going into the shack, only that they'd seen it from the air, and that it was open enough on the roof that they could see inside.

They didn't have to wait long to see what was going on. The two men stood on either side of the building and pulled a large tarp, one that looked like a building had been painted on it, off to reveal a large, brand-new building. The stone walls were still pink, and the mortar was still a nice, pristine white. Misha could not understand why no one would have come out here to investigate. They would have found this much sooner and ended this.

As the men went inside the building, Carter and he moved to the space just below the closed window. They had to be careful not to give away their position, as the men inside might be more than just the two. There was no reason to be stupid at the end of the game.

Rider was on his way with bags of clothes for them all and also some guns. Misha felt sorry for his brother carrying all that extra weight. But it was his turn, and if anyone had to do it, he was sort of glad it was him. Rider was driving him nuts being so smothering.

Within minutes of his arrival, all five of them had shifted and dressed. Misha was strapping his gun to his hip when the door suddenly opened. *Show time,* was the first thing that popped into his head as he drew his weapon.

The wolf came out with his nose in the air. Misha knew it was finally coming to a head, and they had to act now or someone was going to get hurt. Going up behind the wolf, he fired once in his head and let him drop as he turned with his weapon pointed at the building.

The human came out when they told him he was surrounded, but he started shooting almost as soon as he cleared the door. The small gun didn't hit much more than the leaves on the trees around them, and when he was dry firing, Rider grabbed him by the shoulder and threw him to the ground. It just happened to be nearly on top of the wolf. He tried to get up several times before Misha told him to lay still.

"You killed him? You fucking killed him? Mother fuck." Rider told the man that they had and to shut up. "What is wrong with you people? I would have given you a cut of her insurance. Mother fuck, mother fuck. I'm going to have to start all over now, and do you know how hard that's going to be?"

Misha looked at Andrew to see if he was recording this. At his nod, Misha walked over to the man and picked his head up off the ground, much the same way the man had done with the woman earlier.

"Start over?" The man started to struggle, so Misha pushed his head into the dirt until he stopped. "Start over with what?"

"Finding a sadist, you stupid mother fucker. They don't just grow on trees, you know. Do you know how many we had to kidnap before Gunn could get enough practice in so that my wife would suffer? There is double the insurance for murder, and we needed to make sure that it looked like she'd been murdered and not just had an accident. How the hell else was I supposed to pay him back? Gunn was expensive. My mother fucking cunt of a wife is going to suffer like I have all these years."

The sirens sounded in the distance and the whoop-whoop of the chopper was coming closer, the sound getting louder and louder with each turn of the blade. Misha stood up just as Phillip came out of the building. He was shaking his head.

Misha looked down at the man. "I'm afraid you're out of luck, buddy. Your wife is going to live for a while longer."

Twenty-nine hours later, they were boarding a plane to head home. One stop and he'd be in his own bed tonight, and Misha was looking forward to waking when he wanted, not because of a case or an alarm.

~~~

"That'll be twenty-seven dollars and fifty-four cents." Hannah Oliver watched the very smartly dressed woman look at her. She hadn't blinked once since she'd told her the first time how much her meal was going to be. Han, as most people called her, knew just how she felt. Thirty bucks for a meal for two was a shit load of money. And that didn't even count the two coffees she'd gotten from somewhere else in the big airport.

"That's too much." Han didn't even bother arguing with her. She'd heard it all before and figured that was the price you had to pay if you didn't eat before getting on this side of your flight. Once you passed those security guys, you were stuck until you left. "You'll get me the manager right now."

"He's not able to come up here now." Which was true. He was having a nice little nap like he did daily when he came in. "But if you'd—"

The woman slapped both her hands onto the counter, and Han took a step back. She'd been hit before and knew the look of a person who was about to show their mean side. Not at work, of course, but she knew the look of meanness. "Miss, you'll have to back up now. I can't help you if you don't."

"You aren't helping me now, you stupid bitch. I just got into trouble for having too high of an expense account on these trips. You'll either give me the right prices or I'm going to knock you around until you do. I'm not having some high school dropout get me…you're nothing but a minimum wage flunky, and I'm a professional here who holds down a fucking job. Not a burger-flipping bitch who thinks she can cheat me by charging double for this shit. Do you have any idea how long I've been traveling just this week? I'm tired, but I'm not fucking stupid." Her fist connected with Han's jaw before she could move out of the way of it. Her lip felt as if the woman had used a bat rather than her fist. Han put her hand on her mouth to stop the bleeding. She'd be charged if she had to have a replacement uniform again.

The man behind the woman grabbed her as she started over the counter. Han wasn't sure what she would have done if she'd gotten to her. Curling into a ball and hoping for the best was what she normally did, but she doubted that this woman would continue hitting her after she'd lost consciousness, as happened when she was at home. But the man saved her from finding out.

He had the woman's arms pinned behind her back while on her knees in front of him. Han watched him as he held her as if she were nothing more than a bothersome flea. When he asked Han if she was all right, she nodded once, then shook her head.

"Has anyone called security, honey?"

Han's boss chose that moment to come out of his office just as her savior asked her. Dick was a big man in that he had a girth that was as wide as she was tall, and he was as stupid as the bagels that they served. He said that he would call.

Security arrived about five minutes later. Han was sure it was due more to the fact that they wanted free refills on their coffee rather than coming to the call. These two men were what gave most security firms a bad name...lazy, fat, and incredibly stupid.

"You okay?" She took a step back from her rescuer when he reached for her. "I just wanted to make sure you didn't need stitches. May I look please?"

Han nodded and closed her eyes when he touched her mouth. The pain wasn't the worst she'd had, but it still hurt. She knew that he could tell she was afraid of him, but he never said anything. He pressed a wet cloth over her lip and she opened her eyes.

"You need stitches. Four or five I would bet." He took a step back from her when she realized she was blocked by the coffee machine. "I won't hurt you. You have to believe that."

"Mary, you're going to have to finish your shift before you can go anywhere. Maybe next time when you have a problem with a customer you'll let me handle it rather than you trying to be pissy with them. We've talked about your attitude before, haven't we?"

She wanted to remind him that his talk with her had been him trying to get her to blow him. He'd been so pissed he'd only put her on the schedule for four hours one week. But it hadn't worked out. She was the only one who knew how to turn on most of the equipment, including the register. He'd revised the schedule when he had to delay opening the store for nearly three hours before she was able to come in.

Dick told her to get back to work and be thankful she still had a job. He also told her he might write her up just because he could. She looked at the man when Dick left them.

"You have any trouble with him, you give me a call." He handed her a card, and she took it without thinking. "You should just go and get those stitches before it gets too swollen. I bet he uses the wrong name all the time when he talks to you, right?"

"He does." For the briefest of moments she wanted to smile at the man. No one, not anyone, had ever been this nice to her before…at least not in a very long time. When he turned to the other side of the counter from where they were, she saw that there were three other men dressed as he was. She knew that they were all related, too. They had a look…one that she recognized as more than friends. She looked at the man again. "If you get on the other side, I'll take your order. That is if you'd still like to eat here."

He stared at her for a few seconds before he nodded. That's when she noticed that his shirt said "Lanning Search and Rescue." It explained why he'd helped her. It wasn't because he thought she needed it, but because it was as much a part of his job as breathing. She backed up when he took a step toward her.

"You're very skittish, aren't you?" When he moved to the other side of the counter, she took their order and tried to ignore their antics. They were very nice, but nice men didn't like her.

After her shift, she clocked out and went to get her things. Dick called her to his office, but she didn't enter. He had a look on his face like that of a spoiled child, and she wondered what he was up to now.

"I'm letting you go." She nodded, knowing that there was little to nothing she could do now. "I don't need people calling in here screaming at me on how I should treat you. He actually told me that I should appreciate you more than I do and that I should fucking learn your name. Well, Hannah Oliver, you're fired."

She took the sheet he handed her and picked up her things. She was to the bus stop before she realized that her mother was going to kill her. Han didn't know what to do, but got onto the bus to go home, trying to think of any way to tell her mother that wouldn't get her hurt. There was nothing. Han was in so much trouble.

CHAPTER 2

"You okay, honey?" When she looked up at him, Billy saw the wound on her mouth. "Your momma do that to you? Someday you're going to have to hit her back. Then she'll take notice that you're not a punching bag."

Han had been riding his route since he'd taken it from the man before him. She was as regular as a clock and just as quiet. But today he could see the tears she was holding onto. Billy could also smell his friend on her. He smiled when he thought of Carter and what he might have done with a woman like this one. She was not really his normal kind of date, but Billy thought it would be good for the both of them.

When she spoke, Billy was surprised, he thought, as much as she was. "He fired me. I didn't do anything wrong, and now I don't have a job. What will Mother say?"

She seemed to know she'd said too much and snapped her mouth closed. He watched her crawl back into herself as she stared out the window. Billy decided that he'd check on her later, maybe even bring Carter by and see what he might know about the beautiful woman.

Billy had been curious about the young girl for years. She'd get on the bus with bruises, and a couple of times he'd had to help her out of the seat once she got to the airport. She never said much and was always very polite to him when he asked her something. But this was different; even at his advanced age, he could see this time she was terrified.

After he let her off in front of her house, he drove out the rest of his shift. He didn't even bother going home but made his way to Carter's house. The more he thought about young Han, the more worried he got.

He'd heard rumors about the girl. Most of them he knew to be untrue, but there were a couple that had him wanting to pull her aside and have a long talk with her. She'd been in and out of the mental hospital since she'd been about ten, and her mother, a sorrier excuse for a human than he'd ever seen, was right there at the stop with her after she'd been released to tell him all about it. He'd listen to her because he had to, but he was seething inside every time he thought of how much she seemed to enjoy humiliating the poor girl.

The rumor that he'd heard about her first was that she'd seen something. A man had turned into a large wolf right before he'd been killed. The wolf had grabbed her up and saved her from being raped by a few of her mother's friends. According to Han, he'd been standing in his yard, hoeing out his vegetables, when he'd seen her coming.

Billy knew the man, of course. You weren't a shifter in a town this small without knowing who was who. Billy, like his buddy Carter and his family, was a leopard. But unlike them, Billy wasn't the creamy-spotted kind, but a full black one. And just as Han had said, Donald Gamer was a wolf.

Donald had been a very nice man, and Billy could see him doing just what Han's mother had said. Her daughter had told the doctors that a big wolf had saved her, and that had gotten her into trouble. But Donald had been killed when he wouldn't turn the girl over to the men. He had shifted back to human before the police had arrived after he was dead, right along with the other wolf he'd killed protecting the child. Poor Han had been shoved into a shed but had seen the entire thing. The brutality of the event had more than likely been very hard on the child.

Then Han's mother had come to him about a week after he'd started on his new route to warn him about the girl. She was insane. She had issues. And worst of all, her mother had told him, she was a liar. Billy had nodded and said nothing.

But he knew better now. He knew then that what she'd seen was fact, but he didn't know the girl then. Now his heart broke for her every time he let her off in front of that house. But today he was going to do something about it.

~~~

Han walked up the sidewalk seeing that someone, her mother more than likely, had dug up all the flowers again. She'd saved and saved to buy them, only to have them ripped out every year. Han moved to the front of the house and knocked on the door. Someday she'd have her own house, she thought, and there would never be a lock on it for her to be locked out. An impossible dream, but one she cherished. She stood there for a moment before she moved inside when her mother opened the door.

Her mother was a drunk. And if that wasn't bad enough, she was an abusive one as well. Even though Han was twenty-five years old, she'd never be able to get away from her. Her mother was forever telling her that no one would want her, no one would take her in, and she'd never be worth more than the shit she threw in the trash at work. The work she no longer had. She would do as her mother told her because Han was simply terrified of being locked up again.

Han was depressed all the time. And yes, that one time she had tried to kill herself, but she'd been stupid to get caught at it. Not that she'd try again, but some days there was just…. No, Han thought, she was over that stuff. But now her mother had something else to throw into her face…how she'd even been a failure at that. Han tried not to think of it as a failure but as a learning experience.

She moved into the house when her mother told her to shut the fucking door. Han wanted to go to her room, but there was dinner to fix, as well as cleaning up any mess her mother might have made while she'd been gone.

Han went to the kitchen and heard the click-click of her mother's heels overhead as she moved from the bathroom to one of the other rooms up there. Han slept downstairs in the small parlor that served as her room. It had a door and a smallish closet, but it was clean and hers…at least as much hers as it could be living there. She began to pull out things to make for dinner, trying to figure out how to tell her mother that she'd been fired.

Han's was the only income they had. Her mother could have found a job if she'd wanted, but everything was too beneath her, or the timing just wasn't right. Han never brought it up about how poor they were. It had gotten her a good beating when she'd been sassy, as her mother had said, so Han let it go. Her mother spent Han's money like she had a job. And if it wasn't for Han's job and the fact that she paid the rent at the end of the month, they'd have been out on their butt's years ago.

She was making salmon patties when her mother came into the kitchen. Han felt the hair on the back of her neck dance when she was close like this, but she didn't turn.

There was no point in it. Han knew just how she was dressed.

Her hair would be hanging down in a long curl that was more suited to a girl than a grown woman. Her makeup, thick and dark, would be there to hide any signs of aging, which somehow was also Han's fault. Her earrings would be sparkly, long, and gaudy, and would look like heavy weights on her ears. And her dress would be one of three.

There was the blood-red one that was slit up the side to show off her legs. The back was held together by safety pins that had been painstakingly hidden in the stitching because she was forever taking it in or letting it out. The frayed elbows would be covered with an equally red shawl that served only to hide the shabbiness of the clothing.

Then there was the blue one. Han liked the color, but it was all wrong for her mother. Where her skin was a pasty white, the dress only made her look washed out and almost dead. It was similar to the red one in that it was held together by safety pins, but it was less worn because she'd had it the least amount of time. Other than that, it was still skin tight and showed every bit of fat her mother claimed she had.

Pink wasn't her mother's color, either. It, too, washed her out, but instead of making her look dead, it gave her the appearance of pork that had been left out too long. She looked more like one of the dead people in those shows on television than a living, breathing person. This dress was a little more modest than the other two. There was no slit up the side, but it did plunge down in the front so that it showed off her navel and a good deal of her breasts. Han and her mother had nothing in common when it came to chests. While her mother was small and tight, Han was large-breasted and full.

She was also taller than her mother. A good deal taller. In her stocking feet, Han stood just under six foot. Her mother was just over five foot five. She'd told Han once that she'd been with a giant of a man whose dick did not match up to his height. Han flushed for days every time she thought of that.

The fish was almost finished when she turned around, and Han could only stare. Her mother had…she had on a new dress, and had dyed her hair as well. There were no words to describe how she really looked.

"I wondered if you'd ever get your head out of your ass and turn to tell me how good I look." Han nodded, not really sure what to say to her. "I gots this today when I was feeling sorry for myself. I think it's perfect."

The dress—she supposed it was a dress, but Han wasn't sure why it would be considered anything less than simply material that had been hung together—was as ugly as anything she'd ever seen. The front was see-through and her nipples were dark against the virgin white material. Even her pussy was showing, and not just from the lack of color, but also the length of the dress. Han thought if her mother bent over, her entire ass would be exposed, as well as anything else that should have been hidden. Han didn't think of herself as a prude, but this was too much.

The color of her hair nearly defied description. There were streaks of pinks and golds in it, as well as blue and purple. How she'd be able to walk down a darkened street without glowing was beyond her. Han could see other colors, too. She stared at her when she turned in front of her. That's when she noticed the shoes.

The heels were at least six inches tall. It was not unusual for her mother to wear high heels, but Han wondered how she could balance on the ones she had on.

And then there were the spikes that seemed to scream to be noticed. Each tip looked as if it had a drip of blood on it. Han looked at her face when her mother laughed.

"You're jealous, aren't you? Who knew that your mom could look so good, right?" Han didn't answer. She wasn't sure how to. "When you go into work tomorrow, you'll have to get an advance on your next check. I have to pay Cecile back for my new doo."

"I can't." Her mother asked her why the hell not. "I got fired today. I mean, he fired me for something I didn't do."

Her mother just stood there staring at her. Han took a step back when she kicked her shoes off and picked them up in each hand. She knew just what she was going to do with them, and Han felt her body start to scream at her to run. But it would be worse if she did.

The slap of the shoe across her face took her breath away. The second time it hit her in the arm, Han tried to grab it, but her hand only got the spikes, and Han screamed. Her mother hit her three more times with the shoes before Han fell to the floor. After that, all she could do was curl into a ball and hope that she would tire soon.

The plate of food hit her, and she felt the burn of the fish as it spread over her face. Han peeled at it, trying to keep it from blistering too much. But her mother just continued hitting her until she suddenly stopped, turned, and picked up a chair.

Han screamed again when it crashed over her ribs, and the feel of them breaking and hitting her lungs was like hot acid being poured over her body. She knew that they'd been broken when breathing became painful enough to make her dizzy. The next time her mother hit her after the chair had done its damage, Han felt the world around her sliding away. She was going to die this time, and she didn't really care.

The cold splash of water woke her, coughing, but Han cried out when she did and looked up at her mother. A large man who visited her mother some nights was standing over her. He was taking off his belt when her mother laughed.

"I'm so worn out that Big Dan is going to take over. And when he's done, you're going to call that boss of yours and beg him to give you back that job, even if you have to let him fuck you on the desk daily to keep it."

"No." She let out a cry as the belt hit her across the back. "No, I don't want to work there, and I won't have sex with him. Please stop."

The pain was too much, but every time she passed out, one of them would wake her with cold water. Han knew that she'd not be able to take much more and simply let her mind drift away. It was hard with as much as she hurt, but she thought of the wolf. The one that had saved her.

She'd been running from her mother and her boyfriends, four of them. They'd told her that if they caught her, she'd be giving each of them head. Han was young, but she knew what that meant. And the thought of having a man's dick in her mouth was sickening, much less four of them. She'd been given a five-minute head start, and she'd taken off almost as soon as her mother had said "Go."

The man had been in his yard with a large hoe in his hand. He'd seen her, of course, and stopped what he'd been doing to stare at her. She looked behind her when the man—she had no idea what his name had been—whistled for her. Han tried to run again, but she was hurting from the beating one of them had given her.

"Come here." She'd tried to back away from his outstretched hand, but he was quicker than her and held her in his arms until she calmed down. "They won't hurt you today."

Han had nodded and took the tomato that he'd had in his hand. When he took her to the small shed behind his house, he'd shut her in and told her to not come out until the police came. She heard him calling them on his cell phone as the other men still searched for her. Then her mother showed up in the yard with two of her men.

"You seen my daughter?" The man had said nothing, but leaned on the hoe again. "She's 'bout this tall and kind of fat. I had her run to the store, but she's gotten lost."

"You were going to kill her and we both know it. I heard of you and your child. A woman like you should be ashamed of herself for treating something as precious as a child like you do." Her mother laughed. "You aren't going to get her. I've called the police, too."

Her mother had taken off, but the two men had stayed. One of them, a giant of a man, had pulled his shirt off, then the other one did as well. That was when the man had dropped the hoe. Han had wanted to tell him he needed it, but before she could do anything, he dropped to his hands and turned into a giant wolf. He tore into one of the men and killed him immediately. The second man, a wolf, too, had shifted, and they'd fought hard before her rescuer had dropped to the ground with a broken neck. By then the police were nearly atop them, and the surviving wolf took off. Han stayed where she was until the police took her out of the shed.

Her mother had denied it all, of course. And when Han had told them about the two wolves, they'd believed her mother over her. The harder Han tried to get them to believe her, the more her mother's story seemed true. Han was sent to the ward for psychiatric help for nearly a year before she'd been released. She'd never told another soul about the wolves after that.

The beatings had stopped. Han laid there for several minutes trying to take inventory of her body. But there was too much for her to know just what they'd done to her. When she saw her mother coming toward her again, Han closed her eyes and heard her laugh.

"If you die from this, think of how much I'll dance over your grave. If you have one. Big Dan is thinking of burying you in the back." She was flipped over, and Han screamed. Then everything went black. She had no idea what she'd hit her with, but it took everything away this time.

Han hoped that she'd never wake. Life was simply too hard to live.

CHAPTER 3

"I know you were around her." Carter nodded, remembering the girl from that morning when they had landed after the search. He also remembered her face when he'd tried to check her wound. Before he could tell Billy that she'd been okay when he left, Billy spoke again. "He went and fired her. I don't know the why of it, but I don't think things are going to go well when she gets home."

"He fired her?" Carter had seen the entire thing between Han and the pissed-off woman who had attacked her. Carter had taken an instant dislike to the boss as well. "What do you mean, about her home life? Her husband is the one that hurts her?"

Carter had also seen the look on her face…the one that told him she was abused, and a great deal. He'd wanted to pull her into his arms and simply hold her. He wished now that he had. A woman was meant to be held, not used as a punching bag.

"Where is she?" Billy told him, and Carter stood up. "Will you come with me? You she knows and trusts; me not so much."

"You gonna go there now?" Carter nodded. "You know that she's human, right? I mean, I want you to go and check on her and all, but…well…."

"But what?" Carter didn't care what Billy's concerns were. He'd gotten the girl fired and he felt badly about that. He reached for his jacket just as Billy spoke again.

"She's got this mom." Carter paused in mid-step and waited for his friend to continue. "She's been known to hurt the girl. Rumor has it she killed Han's daddy, but I don't know that for sure. Miss Bella, as she likes everyone to call her, is Belladonna Oliver. Ever heard of her?"

"No. Should I have?" Carter was torn now. He wanted to help the girl but not get anyone into trouble. He liked the older man and knew that if his employer found out he had someone going to visit one of his riders, he'd more than likely be unemployed, too.

Since Misha had been shot and left for dead last month they'd all been a little on the tense side. Carter knew that his moods had been shorter, too, and he hated the way he felt all the time. But this girl, this woman might be in trouble because of him. Phillip, Rider, and Misha walked into the room just as he was thinking he'd ask one of his brothers to go as well.

Carter told them what had happened both that morning and now. He told them that he wanted to go to see if she was all right and nothing more. Billy told them what sort of person he'd heard the mother was.

"Leave it alone." Rider sat down looking like what he'd just said was law. Carter had to bite his tongue or snap at him, and that would get him nowhere fast. It was getting harder and harder to stay in a good mood around there. Carter looked at Misha.

"She was hurt?" Billy nodded at Misha's question. Then Misha looked at Carter. "You going alone or did you want some company?"

"I don't know." Which was true. While he wanted to help the woman, he didn't want anyone else hurt, especially his family. And he'd been in enough situations to know that even the simplest things could go deadly in a heartbeat.

"I'll go with you." Phillip smiled as he continued. "Maybe she'll be so grateful that she'll want to do all manner of sexual things to my body when I help her."

His head slammed forward with a loud pop. Carter nearly laughed when he saw their mom. She did not look amused. Each of them stood a little straighter and kept their mouths closed so as not to draw attention to themselves. They weren't afraid of her as much as they were worried about upsetting her. She was their mom and she meant everything to them.

"This girl is hurt?" He said he didn't know for sure. "Yet here you all stand with this idiot making crude jokes. What if she's your mate? Would you want someone saying those things about her?"

"No, ma'am. And she's not my mate, but I did have something to do with her losing her job today." Carter saw the briefest moment of disappointment on her face. He wasn't sure if it was because she wasn't his mate or because he'd helped her lose her job. Either way, he was going to make it up to the woman and his mom. She looked over at Misha.

"You're going as well, if you please. Make sure she's okay and safe. You say she lost her job?" Carter told her she had. "Then we have to find her something. Maybe she could work for your bunch answering the phones and all. I can't do it forever, and she might work out."

"She's human, Mom." She nodded, and Misha did as well. Their mom had been human as well when she'd met their father all those years ago. "We'll see to her."

The drive to the house was made mostly in silence between him and Misha. Billy, not one to ever pass up a captive listener, even one that didn't want to prattle on and on, never shut his mouth the entire way to the house. When the truck slowed in front of a house, Carter felt his gut twist.

The police were parked in the yard and street. An ambulance was still sitting with the doors opened to an empty back end when they walked by it. Two of the cops, friends of the family, were standing near the yellow tape keeping the neighbors out. Carter nodded to one of them.

He was afraid. If he'd gotten her hurt or even killed by what he'd done today, he'd never forgive himself. The closer they got to the house, the heavier his heart got, and the slower his steps seemed to be.

"How bad?" Carter was relieved when Misha asked. He could feel his cat move along his skin in a powerful need to fix and protect.

"Beaten pretty badly. The neighbors called it in. Heard her screaming, I guess, and knew it was bad. One of them told me that when the girl is beaten, she rarely makes a sound. We're looking for her mother now." Carter asked if he could go inside. "Yeah, but don't go in the kitchen. They're working on her still."

Carter moved up the two rickety steps slowly. He could smell the blood and urine almost before he stepped onto the porch. He moved into the house only after Misha gave him a gentle but firm push from behind.

The living room looked like something that only a blind person could enjoy. The pink in the room ranged from neon to something that was even gaudier than that...pink furry pillows, pink shag rug, and hurt-your-retinas-pink walls. The decorations, big pink flowers with equally bright green stems, graced the walls. There was even pink in the giant squares of yarn that hung from the back of the couch. The coffee table had been spray painted to match, but whoever had done it hadn't bothered to remove the glass tops and they, too, were sprayed with the ungodly color. Carter felt his stomach lurch. They were directed down the hall when they asked about where the girl had stayed.

The bathroom they passed was done in purples, much in the same manner as the living room as it was too much. It looked like someone had even tried to spray paint the color on the toilet and the seat, and had hit the wall behind it as well as the floor. Christ, he was nauseous and would never have been able to take a piss in that room.

At the end of the hall they stood in front of a closed door. Carter was almost afraid to open the door, but Misha did before he could touch it. Carter took a step back from the room in shock.

The starkness in the room, the sterile whiteness of it, was actually comforting after the excess of color in the other rooms. He walked in just as Misha cleared the doorway.

A white spread fit neatly over a small single bed. The single pillow was also white, but there was a small stain on the center of it. Blood from long ago was all Carter could think.

There were no pictures on the walls, nor a single poster. The dresser was devoid of anything at all…not even a hair brush or a bottle of perfume. The end table had a lamp, a white one with a shade that was so pale a blue that he had to look hard to see it. It was the only color that marred the perfectly pristine room. There was also a book, but it had fallen to the floor or had been put there to hide it. Carter walked over to read the title.

"It's William Wordsworth. In French." Misha picked it up from the floor before taking it to his nose. As he set it back where he'd found it, something occurred to Carter. "Aren't you reading this, too?"

Misha didn't answer him but walked around the room, stopping only to pick up a white sock that had missed the equally white laundry basket. He held it for a long while before dropping it on the small pile of uniform pants and shirts. When he turned to look at him, Carter could see anger and something…something soft on his face.

"How did you meet her?" Carter told him again about the lunch counter. "Did she ask you for help at any time?"

"No. She seemed…I don't know, surprised that I did help. Why?"

Misha moved out of the room and toward the kitchen. They were just loading up the gurney with Han when they entered. Carter's breath caught when he saw her.

"Good Christ." Misha had moved to her side while Carter just stared. It looked like someone had taken a sander to her face, it was so bloodied.

"Is she stable?" The medic told Misha she was and that they were taking her to County General. "I'd like you to take her to Mercy."

The medic was shaking his head even as Misha stopped him from taking Han out of the room. "They won't take her. She's got no insurance and they don't take the uninsured. Plus, they know in a couple of days her mother will be in there to demand that she come home. It won't matter what shape she's in either. They'll let her go with her. But if you want to know the truth, I don't think she's ever beaten her this badly before."

"Regardless, take her to Mercy. I'll go with you to make sure they know she's where she belongs." Misha looked at Carter as he continued speaking. "Follow us in the truck please. I'll call Mom and have her bring me some dinner in case I have to hang around for a while."

"Misha, what the hell is going on?" He moved with the gurney as they started moving out of the house. Carter put his hand out to stop him from not answering him again. Carter could see the anger on his face and was surprised by it.

"She's my mate."

~~~

Misha didn't have to do much more than demand to speak to the hospital administrator to have Hannah admitted. He'd been willing to put down whatever deposit that they wanted in order for her to stay, but it was unnecessary. The administrator, another leopard, was coming toward him even as Misha was asking to see him. Apparently his mom had called him first. Now Misha was sitting in the waiting room waiting for the surgery to be finished, then for her to be sent to a private room.

"What do you know about the poor girl?" Misha looked at his mom. He'd forgotten she'd decided to stay with him to wait. "Rider said he'd look into the mother as well. Do you think she did this?"

"That's what the medic said. He told me that she was beaten on a regular basis but never like this. And I don't know any more about her than you do. She's twenty-five, years of instability, in and out of mental hospitals, and years of abuse. And according to some records he's already found, she gives as good as she gets." His mother huffed. "You heard what Rider said. That's one of the reasons her mom has her put away. Her violent temper."

"Then I cannot wait to see what this mother looks like now." Neither could he. Misha had seen the girl when she'd been in the ambulance. Someone had used a belt on her back. There was so much damage done there it would be hours before she would be completely stitched up.

Misha leaned back in his chair. He wasn't very good at waiting. And he would admit to only himself he'd rather just leave her there and have someone call him when she was out. But she was his responsibility now, and he took it very seriously.

"You seem awfully calm about finding your mate. Aren't you excited that she's finally going to come into your life?"

He looked at his mom and thought about lying to her, but didn't think she'd appreciate that any more than she would the truth.

"No. What would be the point? We're fated. We met. End of story. Fighting it or being excited isn't going to make it any less so. Ignoring it won't make it go away, so I might as well deal with it and her." She started to speak, but he stopped her by putting up his hand. "I won't hurt her unless it's to calm her. I'll give her whatever she needs in the form of support and help, but she won't have my heart, Mom. I've seen firsthand what that can to do a person."

"Not all mates are like your father and I were. Some live for years and years happily and in love. Don't let what happened to me and him sour you."

Misha didn't say anything. What would be the point?

"Misha, please don't go into this with a shield around your heart. She may fall in love with you."

"Then that would be her loss." Misha closed his eyes, hoping that his mom would leave it alone. He didn't want to talk about his mate and what she may or may not do.

His dad hadn't wanted a mate...wanted children less, he supposed. Every time he sired a son, he would spend a little less time at home and more with his buddies. It wasn't until Phillip had been born that he'd told them he wasn't returning until one of them had something to offer him. Misha had no idea what that might be, and after twenty-four years, he didn't really care anymore.

After dozing for a while, Misha woke to find himself alone. There was a note on his shirt from his mom telling him she'd gone for tea. Misha stood up to stretch and made his way to the nurse's station. Hannah had been in surgery for well over two hours, and he was curious as to how much longer they would be.

"She's in recovery now, Mr. Lanning. Your mom said she'd wake you when she returned. Miss Oliver hasn't been out long, ten minutes I think. The surgeon was able to remove the shards of metal from her cheek and repair any lasting damage she might have had. He said that she will have very little in the way of scars. Her back...." She pulled up the chart and read it before continuing. "There was a great deal of old and newer scar tissue there that he was also able to repair. He notes here that she had been beaten severely before, but no work was done to close some of the deeper cuts. Doctor Hudson said that was what took him the longest, stitching up the places where he had to cut away her old scars."

Misha wasn't surprised that she'd been beaten before last night, but he was that she'd gotten no care. According to what Rider had found so far, she'd been treated every time when her mother had been. He frowned and thought about all the things this was telling him when his mom touched his shoulder. He told her what the nurse had said.

"Then I'll go home." She started away when he told her he'd go as well. "You won't stay here with her?"

"No. I have things to do and sitting around waiting for her to wake won't get them done. I have a couple of the younger ones from the leap here, but there is no reason for me to be here when I have things to do."

"Misha, she's going to need someone here to explain to her what's going on. She's going to wake alone and hurting. You don't want to be here for her?"

"Mom, I'm sure she's done this countless times. I have to go to the office and finish paperwork on our last case. She'll be fine. As I've said, there will be others here if she needs them." His mom huffed, and he smiled. "You should get that taken care of. It sounds very serious."

"I hope she gives you a wonderful time with this. And in the event you don't understand me, I'm being sarcastic." He told her he'd gotten it but wasn't worried. "She's going to make you dance a jig around her, and I'm glad I'm going to be here to see you fall flat on your face. You're going to be so twisted up over her you're not going to know which way is up."

"Never."

Misha took his mom home and then drove to the office. He wasn't surprised to see two of his brothers' trucks there and went inside, closing his door behind him to his office. He was hoping for some peace and quiet, and knew that so long as his door was shut, they'd give it to him. He was sitting at his desk when he realized he'd left his phone in the car, but remembered that he'd given the nurse his office number as well if they needed him. Pulling up the first of many reports, Misha set to work.

He was deep into the last report when his brother touched his mind. It wasn't a soft and gentle touch, either.

Rider was frantic and upset. Misha stood, reaching for his coat even as he answered him.

Mother fuck, where the hell are you? He told him he was on his way in. *The hospital has been trying to reach you for over thirty minutes. The fucking mother is here and she's demanding that we wake her daughter and let her go home with her. Shit, Misha, this is all wrong, way wrong. You should see this...person.*

I'm coming. Just...don't let her go with her. Misha backed out of the parking lot. *I didn't have my cell, but they had the office number. I was right there. Why didn't they try that?*

The service is on. When Phillip left, he said he turned it on and it wasn't until he was in the lot that he realized you were still inside. Where is your cell? Misha looked at it and saw that he had messages but not how many. *Get here now. She's going to hurt Han if she tries to get her into the car she's here in.*

As soon as he was in the lot, he ran to the front entrance. Misha went directly to the floor that Han had been transferred to and got off the elevator in time to see three big men moving the bed that Han was still in toward him. He stepped in front of the bed to stop them, and one of them actually growled at him.

"You don't want to fuck with me, buddy. I've had bigger than you for a snack." The man was either stupid or just...well, stupid. When he rolled up his sleeves on his shirt and took a step toward him, Misha slammed his fist into his face, letting all of his cat help him. The man fell on his ass and didn't move. Misha looked at the other two. "You want some of me, you'll have to wait. I have to get Miss Oliver back to her room."

"You ain't taking my little girl nowhere." Misha looked at the woman who came toward him. A quick glance at his brother Rider behind her confirmed to him this was the mother. "She's gotta get herself home and get another job. I'm not in any shape to make any money and she's gonna pay me back for caring for her. Get on out of the way."

"I don't think so." She put her hands on her hips and glared. "I don't think you understand how injured she is. She needs to have care so that—"

"I know how hurt she is. I was there when we did it, dumbass." Misha looked at the security team that was standing behind Carter. The woman had just confessed to nearly killing her daughter. "I had to do something. She was hurting me."

"Hurting you? You look just fine to me." She smiled at him, and Misha felt his belly jump. She was a predator, more dangerous than he was. When she ran her hand down her body and moved toward him, he took a step back. "Stay away from me."

"You don't want some of this? I assure you, I'm much more experienced at pleasing a man than my daughter is. Besides, she's not right in the head." She looked down at Hannah and sneered. "I had hoped this time that.... Well, that didn't happen."

"What didn't?" She shrugged, and Misha put his hands on the end of the bed and shoved it toward Rider. He took the bed and started own the hall again. Mrs. Oliver looked at him like she was going to claw his eyes out.

"You ain't gonna be able to keep me from my little girl, you know. I gots rights and she is coming home with me. I'm calling the police." Misha braced his arms over his chest and waited. "Well? Go and get her."

"No." He watched her as her anger built up. He could see the exact moment when she realized he was bigger than her and she would never win. "You might want to leave here now and take your goons with you. And if you so much as enter this hospital with an injury again while she's here, I will have you jailed on attempted murder charges."

"You can't do that. I'm her caregiver. I gots it in writing that I can take care of her for the rest of her life." Misha was going to look into that as soon as possible. There was no way this woman was giving care to anyone but herself. "How the hell do I make my rent payment and get my hair done if there ain't no income? You gonna pay me for her?"

"Hardly. You are just going to have to fend for yourself." She asked him what that meant. "Get a job and leave Hannah alone."

She started forward again, but one of the goons she'd brought held her back. The man had no idea how he'd just saved her. The instinct to kill her to protect his mate was overwhelming, and he felt his cat race along his skin to be set free. When the elevator closed behind the four of them, Misha made his way to Hannah's room.

The staff was hooking her back up to the monitors. One of the nurses was grumbling about an IV site being hurt, and Misha lifted Han's hand to his mouth and licked the bloodied wound closed. The nurse nodded at him...she understood him as she was a shifter as well, and told him she'd be able to work now. Misha stepped into the hall with Rider and Carter.

"She's going to come back." Misha nodded at Rider as he continued. "There is something else you should know. I've found out something that might interest you. Han saw a shifter once when she was a child. And in turn, she saw him be brutally killed by another one. It's what got her admitted to the hospital in the first place."

"They thought she was making it up." Rider said they thought she was insane for believing it. "But no one has since tried to talk to her about it? No one of our kind went to her aid? Surely there was someone at that place that was a shifter that could have helped."

"If there was, they didn't come forward." Rider looked at Han, then back at him before he spoke again. "She's your mate and you left her here to be hurt again. Why?"

Misha felt bad enough, and he didn't need his brother telling him he'd fucked up. Instead of answering his question, even if he'd had an answer, he told them he was there now and for them to go home. Neither said anything, but Rider left. Carter sat in the chair on the other side of the bed from Hannah and ignored him. Misha took the other chair and sat down. It was going to be a long night.

CHAPTER 4

Maribel Lanning looked at her future daughter-in-law. She'd been in the hospital for three days now and had not once moved. The nurses came in a couple of times a day and rolled her from one side to the other, but Maribel wanted her to wake up. She had no idea why she thought that the girl and she would get along, but she wanted them to. Putting down her knitting, she stood over the bed and took her hand.

"My dear, I'm so sorry for what you'll have to endure with Misha. He's a good man, but he's had his heart frozen over by his daddy and he is determined not to let you in. I hope you can make him see reason and love him." Maribel sat back down but held her hand still. "My sons will protect you now. You've no worries on that score, I promise you."

The door behind her opened and Maribel turned to look at the nurse. She'd been in their leap, their group of leopards, for about two weeks now. Maribel smiled at her when she told her that she was going to check Han's pressure. They'd been doing that every couple of hours since she'd been brought to this more private area of the hospital.

When Carol left, Maribel picked up her knitting and started on the next row. As soon as she had the count right, she heard a noise and looked up. Han was turning her head toward her.

"Who's there? Mother?" The fear in Han's voice made Maribel's cat stir to protect, but she calmed her. "I can't see. I can't see." Maribel stood up and took her hand. Han latched onto her hard and fast.

"I'm Maribel Lanning. You know my son, Carter. You can't see because of the bandages on your face. They will be removing them soon, I think. It's to protect you against infection." Han didn't say anything, so Maribel continued. "You're in the hospital at Mercy General. You were hurt very badly. Do you remember what happened to you?"

"I fell." Maribel didn't comment on the lie. It was more than likely something Han said a great deal to others when they asked. "I need to leave please. I don't have a job."

"You'll stay right there until the doctor claims you're fit." Han cringed from her words, and Maribel felt horrible. "I'm sorry, child, I should have a care when I speak. You're not going to be able to leave for some time now. There is a great deal of harm to your body."

"I fell and I need to get home before Mother worries." Maribel could only nod. The poor child was terrified and she could smell it. Instead of talking about her leaving the hospital, Maribel spoke of things that were going on. Things she'd done that day.

"I had to make breakfast for all of them this morning. Six grown men, and they'd rather eat cereal than a good hot breakfast. Each of them can cook, mind you, but they rarely do it anymore. Misha said it's too much work when he can just order out. Rider will cook, too, but he's more of a throw-it-on-the-grill-and-eat-it-from-the-cutting-board eater."

"Where am I?" The question startled her for a moment, and Maribel was worried until Han spoke again. "Mercy won't take me because they say I'm a degenerate. I had a job, but I can't afford the insurance. So, please don't lie to me. Where am I? Have they...did she have me committed again and you're my warden?"

"No, child. You are at Mercy General. You were admitted the day you were hurt and my eldest son is caring for your bills." She started to tell her that she was his mate, but Misha had told her about the wolf she'd seen as a child. "I'm not your warden, but Misha had to go on a hunt and he and his brothers are out of town. He asked me to keep you company."

"I don't know him. Nor Carter. I remember the name Lanning, but...I don't know from where." Her fingers began to loosen on her hand, but Maribel didn't let her go. When her hand fell from hers, she knew that she'd fallen back to sleep. The poor thing. All Maribel could think of was how a mother could treat her own child this way. When she thought she could speak to him, she reached out to Misha and told him she had woken up.

Good. Did she ask for anything? I won't give her the world, but I can get her whatever she needs. Just make a list and I'll make sure she gets it when I can get back. Maribel wanted to tell him she needed him but didn't.

She didn't ask for anything but where she was. I told her. She seemed to think I was her warden. She'd meant it as a joke and had hoped that Misha would laugh, but he didn't. *You aren't going to hurry home, are you? You're not going to talk to her now that she's awake?*

Mom, I don't know if you realize this or not, but I have to work in order to make some money for her. I know I have plenty, but she's going to demand things that are

45

going to cost me. Like a house, and new furniture. Do you have any idea how much that's going to run? And I don't plan on dipping into my savings. That's for if I get hurt.

Like you did before. She'd not meant to bring that up, but he'd pissed her off. *How much good did that do you when you were laying there with all those bullets in your chest? How did it keep you from nearly dying twice? I'm so happy to know that you have your priorities straight, Misha. That will go a long way in making your mate happy you're so frugal when she's sitting all alone at home.* There was silence and she knew that she'd gone too far. But when he spoke again, she felt her heart break just a little.

I didn't ask for this and it's unfair of you to think that just because she's my mate, it's going to change a damn thing. Another long pause. *I have work to do. Make a list of things she wants and I'll see to them when I get back. If she needs it now, contact me and I'll have someone get it for her.*

The connection closing down was akin to a phone being slammed onto the cradle. Maribel looked at Han and wondered if she'd be able to love such a hard man. She wondered if she'd even try.

"I tried my best to shield the others from what I was feeling when their father was around. Misha is so...he could read me better than a book. He will be difficult for you to love, if you ever will be able to, and harder for you to understand. I'm sorry for that as well. I should have taken better care that he never knew what I felt. But...I was so lonely."

Maribel picked up her knitting and finished an entire row with so many tears in her eyes that she wondered how she'd not dropped every other stitch. When she set it down again, she went to the window and looked out. She'd done this a great deal when Misha had been shot.

"The man who tried to kill him was high on something. Misha had been hunting people for a long while and hadn't been able to rest like they usually do when they are on a hunt. The man didn't just kill the women, but he'd do things to them that...well, it was horrific. But when Rider and Misha found him in his own lair, bodies of the dead all around him, the man went off the edge and started shooting. I'm not sure what all happened there. Rider was out, and Misha won't talk about it. I know it was worse than that, but.... The man was dead, and he said that was enough. But there is more, much more, and when he finally has to deal with it, it's going to be terrible for him. Misha has...I know you won't believe this, but he has a tender heart."

Maribel turned to the bed and watched the girl sleep. She was her only hope, and Maribel was going to make sure that she helped her son. And in turn, maybe the others as well. They were all hurting and there wasn't anything she could do about it.

Three hours later, Han woke again. This time she was screaming and it was all the nurses could do to get her to calm down. Finally they gave her something to get her to sleep, and Maribel held her hand once again. She didn't even bother telling Misha, but he called not long after.

"Is she all right?" Maribel wanted to ask him why he cared but told him she was fine. "I felt her fear. I don't know what happened, but for a time there she was terrified of something so badly that I had to keep from shifting in the middle of a meeting. But she's okay?"

"They had to sedate her. She'd woken up screaming and they couldn't calm her. But she's fine now." He started cussing, and she let him. There was only so much she could do from there. "Is there anything else?"

He was quiet for a long few moments before he spoke. "You weren't going to tell me, were you? Why not?"

"I'm sure you know the answer to that as well as I do. You simply don't want to care for her, so why should I waste my breath in telling you that she's hurting? I'm taking care of her until you get back, and I get to judge when you should know something or not." He was pissed, and as his mom, she knew it. But right now, Maribel didn't care. "Oh, and you can shove your list up your ass, son. If she wants something, I'll make sure she has it."

Maribel took great satisfaction in hanging up on her son. She rarely got the last word in and it felt really good. As she sat there thinking about how much fun that had been, she looked at Han when she squeezed her hand.

"You should call him back." Maribel started to ask her why when she spoke softly. "He could die this time and your last words will haunt you for the rest of your days."

Maribel picked up the phone twice to call him back. Han didn't say anything else, but she did drift in and out of consciousness for the rest of the night and well into the morning. Maribel never left her side, nor did she let go of her hand. The child was going to mend things, she just knew it.

~~~

Han opened her eyes and tried not to panic. It was still dark to her and that frightened her more than anything. She kept thinking of being locked in a cell with the lights off and she had to breathe through it, telling herself she was okay. The warm hand holding hers was what kept her from screaming again.

Moving her body slowly, Han took a slow inventory of herself. She was hurting, but she also knew that as soon as her mother came for her—and she would—Han would have to be able to move to leave or suffer more. Her leg was heavy, so she figured she was in a cast, and her left arm was heavy as well. Not like her leg, but still weighed down.

Breathing hurt, and she tried not to think about not coughing, a sure way to induce a coughing fit, because she knew from past experience that she'd hurt more when and if she did. Broken ribs were as much a part of her life as wearing shoes. When she tried to turn her head, she felt the pain in her back and cried out from it.

"You have over ninety stitches in the upper part of your back, and at least that many more along your legs and thighs. I would suggest that you lay very still for a few more days." The man's voice startled her and she pulled her hand away from who she had assumed was the woman. "Do you need anything?"

"No." He laughed and she felt her temper rise, but she kept it back. "When will they take the bandages off my face?"

"Today, if you can stay awake long enough. They want to see if your eyesight was affected by whatever it was she hit you with. What was it?" She told him she fell. "Of course you did. And when you fell, did you happen to have a leather belt in your hand that you hit yourself with over and over, too?"

Han didn't like his tone but said nothing. She had a feeling he knew a great deal more than she did about what had happened. After she'd passed out, she remembered flashes of someone talking to her about what had happened, but she knew better than to answer those types of questions.

"They still have an IV in your arm that's giving you something for pain and some juices or something to keep you from being starved. They said you could have some ice chips. I can get you some if you want them." She told him no thanks. "You're going to be stubborn, aren't you? Well, it won't get you anywhere with me. You want something, I would suggest you stop playing around and tell me what it is. I'm not going to try and guess at what you want all the time."

Han turned away from his voice and said nothing. She wanted to be left alone, but she doubted that he'd leave. Instead, she lay there thinking about her last book. She wondered if her mother had found it and if she had, did she tear it up like she had a few of the others she'd gotten.

The man started talking again and she realized that he was on a phone. Han felt her body begin to mellow out again and wondered if someone had slipped her more drugs. Just before she let sleep take her again, she heard a door open, then close.

"She's awake but not talking to me." The woman's laughter made her smile a little. It was the woman from before and she found her laugh to be so soothing.

"You more than likely pissed her off, too. What did you say?" He relayed the conversation she'd had with him, and the woman laughed again. "Misha, do you ever think before you speak to someone? Why did you assume she wants something from you the first time you speak to her?"

"Everyone wants something from someone. It's the way of the world. But I'm not going to go around buying things for her to try and placate whatever weird woman ideas she has about me." Han wanted to tell him to fuck off but kept her mouth shut. She didn't want to get hit again right now. "I have to go out for a minute. Will you stay with her?"

If the woman answered, Han didn't hear it. When the door opened and closed again, she hoped that it was the man and not the woman leaving. He was a prick, and Han decided that she didn't like him.

"Will you speak to me?" Han turned to the soft voice. "I'm thinking you simply don't know what to say rather than not speaking to him. Am I right?"

"I don't want him to hit me." She didn't know why she'd said that to this woman, but she felt like she could talk to her. "When do you think I can leave? I have to find a job."

"You will be coming home with me when you're released. The boys, my sons, all have a place of their own in the house but nothing that they actually own. Misha is looking into houses now. What do you prefer in a home?"

"Safety." Again, Han had no idea why she'd said that to her but changed the subject. "He said they were going to take the bandages off today if I stayed awake. Do you know...can you tell me how to tell them I'm awake now?"

"I will take care of that for you." She heard the woman move about the room. Then she heard her talking to someone. When she hung up the phone, she came back to her. "I don't know if you remember me telling you my name or not, but I'm Maribel Lanning. You're Hannah Oliver, correct?"

"Yes." Han moved slowly on the bed so that she could stretch out her good leg. "I don't know why I'm here. Shouldn't I be at County?"

"You're here because my son made arrangements for you to be here. He wanted you to have the best care possible." Han didn't understand that at all. The man she'd met seemed to wish her gone. Han hadn't realized she'd spoken aloud until Maribel spoke. "He doesn't want you gone, but he doesn't understand you. You're something new for him to deal with."

"I want to go home, not be dealt with." The door opened again, and she heard several people this time. One of them had a deep voice and said his name was Doctor Hudson. He also explained what he was going to do.

"I'm going to take the bandages off slowly. I don't think there is any reason for them to hurt, but there might be a few sticking places. I want to give you something for pain now so that when I get closer to your skin, it will already be working."

"No. Please. No drugs. They cost a great deal and...." She didn't want to cost any more than she had to. She'd eventually have to pay this man back, and she was pretty sure it was already a fortune. "I'll be fine."

The first layers of gauze, he told her, were just there for padding. As he got closer and closer to her actual skin, Han could see more light. When he paused for several seconds, she knew that someone else had come into the room.

"Is she hurting?" She knew the voice and tensed up. She moaned a little before she could stop it, and he spoke again. "Give her something, damn it. She's too stubborn to ask for anything on her own. She's trying to piss me off, that's all."

"Get out of here." She heard her voice and almost didn't recognize it, but she was mad, too, now. "Get out of here and don't you dare come back. I hate you."

There was a sharp intake of breath, then silence. She could hear things moving around and then the door opening again. Someone took her hand, and she pulled back. The laughter made her think it was Misha again.

"It's Carter Lanning. You and I met the day you were slapped by the broad at the counter." She still didn't let him take her hand. "You know, I think you might have been able to handle her on your own. You sure did Misha."

"He's a bully." Carter laughed, and she felt herself relax a little. "I want you to keep him out of here. He thinks...I don't know what he thinks, but I don't want him around me again."

"That might not be possible, love. I'm pretty sure that he's going to be hanging around you a great deal from now on. And I think you two might be more suited than I first thought." He laughed again, and the doctor told them it was time to finish. He asked her if she wanted anything for pain and she told him no. She would do this now even if she had to suffer for days.

The light was blinding when he got to it, but someone turned the lights down and it got a little better. She knew she must have looked horrible, and the look on the face of the man next to her confirmed it. She asked them all to leave her, please. Everyone left but Carter.

"You look better. Not to say you look perfect, but you look better than when I saw you at your house." Han didn't say anything. Her mother had beaten her badly this time, and Han was terrified. Carter sat down on a chair with the back to his chest. He stared at her for a long time.

"You should leave now." He nodded but didn't move. "I don't know what's going to happen to me now, but I'd very much like to be alone to make some arrangements."

"You're not going to like me any better than you do Misha when I tell you what's going on." She turned from him and tried not to cry. She had a feeling she wasn't going to like very much of anything that happened to her from now on. "You're not going back to your house, and no one is going to put you in a mental ward. Not if I have anything to say about it."

"She can." Han turned to him when he didn't say anything. "She's had me declared unfit to live alone. I can't do anything but what she tells me to do. I'm not…I have a mental issue."

"Don't we all." She thought he was trying to be funny, but it wasn't. He looked at her. "No one is going to hurt you again, Han. I promise you this. Misha is upset, yes, but he'll never hurt you."

"Why does he figure into my life?" She could tell he was hiding something, and she didn't press. If she wasn't supposed to know, it was more than likely for the best. "I want you all to leave me alone. I don't know how I'll pay him back for making sure I had good care, but I do appreciate it very much."

"*Que ferez-vous quand elle vous fait mal à nouveau?*"

Han answered his question in the same French that he'd asked her with. She didn't know what she'd do when her mother hurt her again. Deal, she supposed. "*Je vais faire de mon mieux et essayer de rester en vie. C'est tout ce que je peux faire.*" Telling him she was going to do the best she could to stay alive was a stupid answer, but it was really all she could do. Turning her head from him, she continued in English. "I'm very tired, Mr. Lanning. I'd very much like for you to leave now as well. Tell your brother…tell him that I'm sorry I lost my temper with him, but…but I'm not being stubborn, just…I'm just me."

"Hannah, look at me." She turned and could see that he was hurt by her words. She was not used to people caring so much about her, but he spoke before she could tell him she was sorry. "My brother is your mate. I know that you have no idea what that means, but it will come clear to you when he talks to you. And you have to let him talk to you. He can keep you safe like no other person can, and he will.... He might be pissy about it, but he will keep you safe."

"I don't want him to." Carter shook his head and stood up. "I'll pay him back for having me cared for, but I don't want him to come here again. It's not necessary for him to. I want to thank you for what you've done for me, both before and now, but I have to do what's right for me."

Carter leaned down and kissed her on the forehead. When he left her, Han lay there for a long time, just thinking about nothing in particular. Then she knew what she had to do. Reaching for the phone with her good hand, she called the only person she knew to call. Her mother. Han knew for some reason that she was going to suffer like she'd never suffered before when she went home this time.

CHAPTER 5

Misha came down to breakfast to find his mom sitting at the table with a half cup of tea in front of her. She was staring off into space, and he reached for her cup. It was as cold as if she'd put ice in it. He touched her arm and called to her twice before she looked at him.

"She's left the hospital." Misha started to stand up, but she told him to sit down. "You have no one to blame but yourself on this, so just sit there and listen to me. Her mother called me about an hour ago to tell me that I was to give you a message. Would you like to know what it is?"

"Yes, please."

Instead of answering him, she stood up and moved to the counter. He didn't say anything as she filled the kettle up with water and set it on the stove. As she moved back and forth between the sink and the stove, he could see that she was getting angrier and angrier with each step.

"Her mother told me that her daughter was going away for a time. I'm just betting where that might be. But she said that I was to never contact them again, and that if we tried to send her the bills, she'd sue us." His mom turned on him so quickly that she splashed tea on him from her cold cup. "Do you know how badly I wanted to jump through the phone and tear her throat out? In all my years as a leopard, I've never once wanted to kill before. Not even your father when he…I wanted to kill her."

"I'm sorry, Mom." She slammed her cup on the table and it shattered. With a quick glance at her hand, he could see that she hadn't cut herself, but he still worried about her. "I'm going to get her to come here."

"And do what? Should she sit around so you can take cheap shots at her? That will make for a wonderful relationship for you both. You snapping at her like she's a child and her hurting because you hate her."

"I don't hate her. I don't even know her well enough to dislike her." That had come out wrong, and he tried to salvage it. "She's my mate. I will do whatever it takes for her to be safe. Her mom won't be able to hurt her again so long as I live. I promise."

"But you still will leave her open to the pain you inflict on her, though." His mom sat down before she continued. "Leave her alone, Misha. I beg of you to. The girl has been through enough without you tearing her apart more. As much as I love you, I want you to be happy, and you won't with her here or even in your life. I know she won't be."

"You think I should just let her suffer at the hands of her mother for the rest of my life?" His mom said it would be better. "Better for who? Her mother? It certainly won't be for her. I didn't see her when they took those bandages off her, but I saw her at the house. Christ, she looked like someone had cut her up and then beat her with something like a cat-o-nine tails. And her back…did you know that her 'mother' used a belt on her over and over until she bled so badly that her back looked raw? Mom, how will she be better off if she stays with her?"

"Her heart will not be torn from her chest."

58

Misha could hear the pain in her voice, see the hurt and anguish on her face, and he wanted to pull her into his arms and hold her. Hold her as she'd done him all those years ago.

"Leave her alone, Misha. It's for the best."

Misha went to his office and sat at the computer for a long time, just staring at it. When he reached for the mouse, he moved it to do a search before he could change his mind. When he found what he was looking for, he called Rider.

"I need for you to see if we have anyone working at the County Mental Board. I need to have a patient reevaluated as soon as possible." Rider asked him if it was Hannah. "Yes. I want…I need to make sure she's okay, and I can't do that if she's not where I can help her."

"Mom said she told you to leave her alone. I think that's good advice. You don't need a mate, and you certainly don't need one that you're going to hurt every time you open your mouth." Misha felt his cat tear at his skin wanting to hurt his brother. "Just fucking leave her alone, why don't you?"

"I can't. I…I tasted her blood and now I can feel her. She's afraid and hurting right now. They'll hurt her there and I will feel every bit of it. When it gets bad, what do you think is going to happen when my cat decides he's going to find her and protect her?"

"Fuck." Misha couldn't have agreed more. "I'll call you back in a bit. You should have told me you took her…when the hell did you manage to bond with her? She's been out or screaming for you to leave her alone since she woke up."

Misha didn't answer his brother. He knew that, really, all he'd done was taste a small bit of her, but it was enough to feel her overwhelming pain. He had no idea if she was hurting now or not, but it got Rider to help him, and he needed that. Misha leaned back in his chair and thought about what he had to do now.

He was looking at a house not far from his mom. It was a nice size if she ever wanted to sell and move in with him, which he sort of hoped she would. Hannah would have plenty of room to do whatever she wanted, and there were plenty of bedrooms that she could have her pick of...so long as it wasn't his. He'd have to explain to her how things were going to go as soon as possible. He didn't love her, he would more than likely never love her, but he might grow fond of her someday. When his phone rang, it was the realtor. Misha took that as a good sign.

The house was his, as were the fifty acres surrounding the ten that the house sat on. His mother's house and her property butted right up against his, so that would be great for them all. More room to run. As he made arrangements to sign the paperwork, he made notes on things that had to be completed. Rider called him ten minutes later.

"I have a buddy that's going to arrange to get in to see her. I'm not saying that he'll be able to evaluate her, but he's going to see her. Mark said that when they have a new patient come in, they do a small question and answer session. I've made it so that you can go as well. If you piss her off, it's going to be finished." Misha wasn't sure he could be around her during this meeting then. They never seemed to get along on the best of terms, and he said as much to Rider. "Then how about Mom goes?"

"Mom?" Misha knew that their mom liked Hannah. And he was reasonably sure that she liked Mom, but how would this meeting go with her there? Given the alternative, she would be better than him. "Okay. But we have to have time to talk to Mom. She'll need to know what to tell her."

"I think Mom can handle more than you can right now." Misha wanted to snap at him but knew, deep down, that he was right. "I'm going to call Mom now and have her tell me when she can do this. Then when I have it set up, I'll call you back. And Misha? Please, just shut up. She isn't going to be happy with this, I have a feeling, and you pissing her off is not going to help her results."

Misha sat in his office for several minutes before he thought about what he was getting into with a mate. She was going to make demands on him that he wouldn't like. Then she was going to be whiney about it. Misha smiled when he thought of her telling him to get out of her room. Someday he thought he might enjoy her standing up to him. Maybe.

~~~

Carter sat in the waiting room and watched the others as they milled around the room slowly. Most, he could tell, had been so doped up that they could barely function. Others, at least two of them, were drooling on themselves, and one of them had shit themselves. This was not a place for Han.

"Mr. Lanning?" He stood up when the nurse said his name. "I just got a call from her doctor, and he said it would be all right for you to visit. But that…I'm to keep it off the books?"

"Her mother." The nurse nodded as if she understood and led him down the long hallway. "Do you know if she needs anything?"

"She needs to have someone come here and take her home. The girl needs someone to love her, not treat her like this." She stopped walking and looked at him, shock written all over her face. "I'm sorry. I didn't mean that. I'm sure that Miss Oliver gets—"

"I think you're right." She nodded, relieved. "I like her. Han, I mean. And I want her to have more than I think she can get here. No offense."

"None taken. We have very little to offer her in the way of support. There's not enough money for the ones that really need to be in here, much less a woman like her." She turned to look down the hall, then back at him. "I know that I shouldn't be telling you any of this but...you being a shifter and all, I know you can see more than most of the people here. Hannah is a wonderful person, but if she doesn't get help soon, and I mean very soon, she'll be right back where she was, and this time her mother will kill her."

"I'm working on that." She nodded and told him which room Han was in. "Thank you for your honesty. I think my brother is working on getting her what she needs."

After she left him, Carter went to the door and knocked. When she said for him to enter, Carter took a deep breath and went in. She was sitting in a wheelchair near the barred-up window.

"I don't know why you're here." He sat down in front of her, moving the chair so that she could see him. When she didn't look his way, he put his finger on her chin and had her turn.

"I like you." She nodded, and he could see the tears. "I wanted to be sure that you're okay. I...I have a friend that works here and she got me in."

"I'm not supposed to have any visitors. I think it's because I'm unsafe." She turned back to the window again. "She's going to kill me when I get out of here. She told me so."

"I'm not going to let that happen." Han nodded but said nothing. "I wanted to talk to you about a few things. I have some time, but I want to make sure that you understand what I'm saying. All right?"

She nodded but still looked out the window. Carter wanted to lift her up and carry her out of there, but doubted he'd get very far. Looking around the room, he wondered how anyone could survive like this. He knew that he couldn't.

The bed and the small stand were both chained to the floor. There was a single chair, the one he was sitting in, but it, too, was chained to the wall, with just enough play in it for him to move it to her and that was it. There was no phone in the room, no lamp, and the drawers on the small stand were padlocked so that only a person with a key could open them. Carter looked at Han.

"You're in prison." She nodded and turned to look at him. "I'm so sorry for this. I had no idea that this would happen when I tried to help you."

"You didn't do anything wrong, Mr. Lanning. It was just a matter of time before she got it in her head to have me come here. It's usually when she's threatened with eviction because she'll use the rent money for a dress or her hair. Then I get committed for a time and she gets her way. I'll be out before you know it."

"You said she'd kill you when you go home. You believe that, don't you?" She looked around the room, then at him before she answered.

"She will. Do you want to know why?" He nodded. "Because I'm not going to let her do this to me again. I'm going to…I'm not sure what I can do, but I'm not going to let her hurt me like this again. Even if I have to spend the rest of my life here, it will be better than what I've endured my whole life."

Carter nodded. He had to tell her some things. Rider and the doctor had given him a list of things that he was to talk to her about before they got there. He pulled out the pictures he'd taken that morning of his cat, as well as the list.

"I'm going to tell you something. Something about my family. I don't want you to get upset or start to scream. Okay?" She nodded and smiled. He smiled back. "I really do like you, Han. You're very special to me. And my family."

"What is it?" He nodded. "Mr. Lanning, before you tell me, I was wondering if you could help me back to the bed. I've been sitting here for over nine hours, and while they have me catheterized, I still hurt to sit for so long."

He felt his cat skim along his skin. She'd been sitting like this for...he stood up and asked her how to do it. When he had her in his arms, he knew that she was hurting, but she told him it was all right. As he placed her in the bed, he reached for his friend and told him to bring her something for pain, but learned that there was nothing prescribed. Carter asked Han about it.

"My mother said it was too expensive and that I needed to get off them anyway. I hurt really badly, but I'll be okay in a few minutes." She wouldn't and they both knew it. Han was as white as the sheet she laid on, and her hands were trembling. "Maybe you could just tell me what it is you have to say. It might take my mind off it."

"You really saw a wolf that day when you were a child." She looked at him, and he felt his face heat up. "I really meant to lead up to that, but I guess I was trying too hard to distract you."

"You did. But really, what did you want?" He sat on the wheelchair and moved it close to her bed. He knew that there were cameras in the room, but they weren't recording sound. Carter decided to start from the beginning.

"I'm a shifter. A leopard actually." He handed her the picture of himself. "They wouldn't let me bring in my camera, so this is all I could show you."

She stared at the picture, and then handed it back to him. "This is supposed to be a joke. You're trying to what, make me feel good about myself before you tear the rug out from under me? This isn't funny, Mr. Lanning. I'd like for you to—"

Carter put his hand on her arm and let his cat shift over him. When his claws moved from his fingertips, he moved his hand off her skin to her sheet and watched as his fur encased his arm. She didn't say anything, but did put her hand out as if to touch him. When she stopped just short of doing it, he pressed her hand over his fur.

"I'm not a full blood, none of us are. My mother was human when she met my dad and he converted her." She stroked his arm, and he purred. Her laughter made him smile. "He likes you. And so you know, I would never be able to hurt you. You're a part of my family now, and it would be impossible for any of us to hurt you."

"The man who...the wolf. He's real as well? I mean, he was real?" Carter nodded, and Han burst into tears. "I really saw him. I really saw him turn into a wolf and kill the other one."

"You did." He pulled his cat back but held her hand. "I have more to tell you if you think you can handle it."

"I'm not crazy." She put her hand over her mouth and the tears continued to flow. "I'm not crazy. I'm as sane as you. You are sane, right?"

He laughed. "I am, I think. I'm so glad you didn't take this badly. I thought…well, I'm not sure what I thought, but I didn't think you'd do so well."

She held his hand tightly and he let her. There would be hell to pay when Misha found out, but Carter figured he needed this as much as she did. When she nodded again, he handed her a tissue and spoke softly.

"My brother, Misha, is your mate. I know that you have no idea what that means, but you're basically his wife." She started shaking her head. "Let me finish, please? I need to explain to you what we can do for you."

"I don't want him around me. He hates me. And…and I don't care all that much for him either." She shook her head and pulled her hand from his. "Tell me the rest, but I'm not going to be his wife. Please don't make me."

"He's your mate, honey. And he is going to get you out of here. When he does, he's going to take you to his home and provide for you. Make sure you're safe, as all of us will do. You'll never have to go back to your mother again. He'll make sure of it." Carter watched her face and could see that she wasn't going to do this. Not for any amount of money. "Misha said that if you do this, he'll make sure you never have to work again, that you'll have whatever you want within reason, as well as his money."

"His money?" Carter nodded. "He thinks…will he want to have sex with me, too? I mean as his wife, that's pretty much a given, right?"

Carter didn't know how to answer her so he said it was a given. "He'll keep you safe. And that should be enough until you love him, right? I mean, he's a pain in the ass most of the time, but he'd never hurt you."

"You think so, do you?" Carter didn't understand the pain that he heard in her voice and tried to think how to fix this. "I'd like for you to finish whatever it is you need to tell me."

Carter nodded. Maybe he'd been mistaken about the pain he'd heard and wondered what was wrong with her, and concluded that it had to be from sitting for so long. So he pulled out his list and started on the things she had to do and say. "You cannot mention the wolf or the cat. When the doctor comes to evaluate you, you'll just answer his questions as truthfully as you can, but don't mention the wolf or my cat."

She nodded at each point, but she never spoke again while he finished up. Carter felt as if he'd lost something in this. Her friendship was…it was important to him that she trusted him. When he asked her if she had any questions, she told him just one.

"If this works, what is your brother going to expect from me? I don't mean…I know he's going to expect something. No one would go to all this trouble for me without something in return. What is it?" He told her that it was his responsibility to care for her and nothing more. "I see. Will you have him make a list of his expectations and have it sent to me?"

"I will." Carter watched her face as she settled back into the bed. He wanted to tell her to forget this. That she might be better off telling them that he'd shifted partially and that she'd seen the wolf. In here she'd be safe, and Misha would…Misha wouldn't hurt her. Because as surely as he was sitting there, Carter knew that Misha was going to hurt her.

"I'll wait on the list then. When you get it…when it gets here, I'll make sure to let you know what I want to do." Carter stood up, but before he could say anything more, his friend came in.

As he left, Carter reached for Rider. He didn't want to talk to Misha just yet and told Rider what she wanted. Rider said he'd ask Misha and make sure she got it.

Does she need anything else? Carter wanted to tell him she needed everything, but told him she couldn't have anything. Then he told him about the chair as well as the pain meds. *I'll have Danny Hudson see that she has better care.*

I'm not going to take her the list. Misha can try to make me do it, but I won't. I don't think I can handle the hurt on her face when he spouts off about what he wants in this, and she gets shit. Rider started defending Misha, but Carter cut him off. *No. She needs this list, and I really can't blame her for wanting to know what's right up front, but I won't take it to her knowing that it's going to hurt her.*

All right. I'll get it to her another way. Other than the meds, did she mention anything else?

Yeah. She's thrilled to death to know that she's not insane.

Carter found himself a hotel for the night. For whatever reason, he simply didn't want to go home just yet. As he lay there on the bed with the lights off, he thought of what he should do. It was time, he realized, past time for him to move into his own place. He was going to start looking as soon as he got up tomorrow. Maybe he'd take that job out west. It was time for some changes.

CHAPTER 6

Misha sat in the waiting room so that he could be close when things went wrong. He had no doubt that they would, either. His mom was pissed at him. Rider, too, but he had a good reason. And Carter was refusing to speak to him. He had too much on his plate right now to be fucking around with their emotions when his entire life hung in the balance.

"The list," as it had come to be called, was making him look like the bad guy. He wanted to blame Hannah for it, but it was his list. She'd only asked for it. Misha actually had thought it was a reasonable explanation of what he expected. Contrary to their beliefs, he did want the same list from her, and he would take each and every one of her expectations under consideration. To his way of thinking, he was the one who had to make the most changes in his life. But he had to admit, he was enjoying having his own home.

His mom was mad at him because of her idea of what he should have said to Hannah. He'd listed things like keeping herself neat and bathing daily. How the hell was he supposed to know that a woman would take offense to that? If she didn't want to know, she shouldn't have asked. He crossed those two things off, but he did leave in that she was to keep out of his bedroom unless he wanted to have sex. To him, that was a good way to convey that this was a marriage only to benefit them both and nothing more. She'd get a house and a roof over her head, and he'd not have to worry about finding a bed partner when he wanted sex. He didn't need it that often anyway.

The other things, like she'd have to ask him for expenses over five hundred dollars, was just smart. He didn't want to be broke within a few months of them getting married. And he was going to marry her.

"I should have beaten you more." He was shocked that his mom said that to him. "Maybe then you'd be a great deal nicer when things didn't go your way."

He didn't understand that and left her in the kitchen. But Rider he'd hit, several times before he finally felt like he'd made his point. He was not going to put her name on anything that he had no control over. There was just no point in having her name on the house, the cars that he worked hard to get, or the insurance policy. What if she had another episode and he had to have her committed? That had earned him a black eye, three cracked ribs, and a bloodied lip. Rider wasn't in any better shape, but now he wouldn't answer his calls when he needed him.

And Carter was leaving them. Misha thought of the phone call he'd gotten before leaving his new house that morning. One of his buddies from college, who worked as a private investigator, had called to tell him he was glad there weren't going to be any hard feelings about Carter coming to work for him. Misha was confused at first, then Scott had told him that Carter was starting to work for him the following Monday.

"It was my understanding that he had your blessing on this." Misha looked at the envelope that he'd found on his kitchen table when he'd gotten downstairs that morning. Had he opened it, like it told him to do immediately, he might not have been blindsided. As it was, he had been clueless until he got off the phone. Not only was Carter leaving Lanning Search and Rescue, but he was moving to the other end of the United States. His mom was, of course, blaming Misha for that decision as well.

"Mr. Lanning?" Misha looked up at the pretty nurse. "Miss Oliver would like a quick word with you before they begin. She said that it's important or she wouldn't bother you."

He felt both stupid and pissed at the same time, and could figure out neither feeling as he moved down the hall to a small room. Hannah was sitting in a wheelchair with a blanket over her arm and leg when he walked in. The door closed behind him as soon as he went inside.

"I've signed your papers." He nodded and took the offered envelope. "I just have one question for you."

"Of course. But if you want to have more, then you're going to have to postpone this meeting. I'm not agreeing to anything without my lawyer writing it up." She nodded. "You want more?"

"No. I just…may I have a job?" He was confused by the question, and she seemed to know it. "I'd like to have a job when I can get around. I would like something of my own. Something I can do without causing you embarrassment."

"Of course. If you have the time that is." She nodded. "What else? Surely you have other demands of me. I'm a very wealthy man, Miss Oliver. But I won't be taken advantage of."

"There's nothing else." He waited for the "But I want," but there was nothing more. When she told him she was ready and asked him to step into the hall so she could finish getting dressed, he walked out. The nurse who had come for him told him to go back to the lobby and wait. Misha was sitting on the couch before he could think to ask her why she really wanted a job. He told himself it was so she could be pitiful, but doubted she'd own up to that.

He was able to get some work done or he might have been in a worse mood when five hours later, Rider and his mother came down the hall. Stuffing everything in his briefcase, he stood up and watched as his mom moved by him to the door. He looked at Rider.

"I think she did well. I was very proud of her for thinking about each question before she answered. She was clear and explained everything to them when they asked, and she even told them why going back to her mother was going to be bad for her. I think she'll be out soon." Misha nodded and when Rider stepped around him, he stopped him.

"When?" Rider looked confused. "When will she be moving into my house? I mean, I need to make arrangements for her."

"They said it would be a week before they had a final determination. If you're interested, she's being moved to a regular hospital within the hour. Apparently someone said something about having someone as injured as her in a long-term facility that provides special care." Misha started to ask who, but Rider answered him first. "I don't know who did it, but I would say it was Carter if I had to guess. He's been visiting her every day, apparently."

Misha didn't know what to say, so he said nothing. Rider left the building a few minutes later, and Misha did as well. He thought about going to see Hannah again but wasn't sure what he'd say to her that hadn't already been said. Instead, he went home and called around for furniture. If she came to his home in the next few weeks, he should have something for her to sleep in. After he was finished, he sat at his computer and tried to get some work done.

It was nearly midnight when Misha stood up. He'd gotten very little done in the hours since he'd been sitting there. More than that, all he'd been able to think about was Carter going to see his mate. He wondered if she was pumping him for information about his account, and doubted that almost as soon as he thought about it. Carter might be mad at him, but he'd never betray him. Misha went up to bed and tried to get some sleep. The call came just after two in the morning.

He rolled out of bed taking notes on the murders even as he reached for Rider and the others. Dressed and packed, he was waiting in his kitchen when the rest of them showed up. Within minutes they were on the road.

"Two women dead and three more missing. They think that whoever this is, he works alone. The bodies of the woman are ours to inspect and they haven't been moved." Misha told them everything he knew as Rider drove. By the time they got to the airport, his brothers knew as much as he did.

Misha tried to engage Carter in some banter as they flew to Wyoming, but he only nodded at him. He felt his heart twist in his chest when he saw him talking and laughing with Phillip and Andrew. By the time they landed, Misha was hurting and he didn't know how to fix it. He finally asked Carter about Hannah.

"We play chess and we talk about books. Believe it or not, you're never mentioned and she never asks about anything you might be doing." Misha doubted that was the case and said that to him. "Then you'll believe or not believe me when I tell you that she's too good for you, and that I really wish you'd leave her alone. Right now it all sounds like it's going to be good for her, but I don't think you've thought this through. She's going to be hurt by this, much like Mom was with Dad."

"I'm not our dad." Carter didn't say anything. "I'm not. He was a bastard that wanted his freedom more than he wanted a family. I've made it perfectly clear that I want no children and that she can be safe with me."

"And that's enough for you?" Misha nodded. "Well, I wish you the best of luck then. I'm certainly glad that I won't be here when the shit hits the fan. Because I've no doubt, big brother, that you're going to regret this more than you can imagine."

~~~

"I don't know what you mean. I can't see my own daughter? Why are you doing this to me?" Bella tried to use her considerable charms on the man at the desk, but he was probably queer or something. He was sneering at her like she was something dirty. "I demand that you let me see her right now."

"I'm sorry, Mrs. Oliver, but the doctor has it stated that she is to have no visitors until he finishes with his write-up. I believe you were notified of the hearing by mail." She more than likely was, but she couldn't get her mail because she had no idea how to get it. Her daughter had done that for them. "There will be a findings hearing on Monday. And if you call in the afternoon, I can have someone give—"

"I don't want her having no evaluating hearing. I want her to get her ass home. I'm better equipped at handling her insane self now, and I can take care of her like she needs."

The man started shaking his head. "You're going to let me go back and see her or so help me, I'll call the police."

He turned the phone her way and told her to press nine to get an outside line. Bella was so pissed off she actually picked up the phone to call them, but put it down. If the police came here looking for trouble, they'd only have to look at her to find it. She was slightly stoned as well, as she'd been having a little too much fun since she'd been on her own. But the rent was due again and there wasn't enough left of the money her daughter had left in her room to do more than rent a movie. Which reminded her, she was going to pick up that new one on the way home. She looked up at the man she'd had bring her here. She had no idea what his name was, but he'd told her he'd bring her here for a quick blow job. She'd have to do that too, and more if she wanted him to take her to the video rental store, too.

"You go and get her then if you won't let me go and see her. That's not breaking the rules now, is it?" She batted her eyes at him, and he shook his head. "Fuck this shit, I'm going back there."

Before she could get around the desk, there were two security guards standing in front of the big door. She might have been able to take one of them, but two? Not really. Giving the guy at the desk her best glare, she went out to the car with her driver.

"I have to go someplace else." He told her she had to pay up first. "Here in the car? You don't want to go somewheres that we can have fun, too?"

"No. I don't want anything more than for you to suck my cock. Do it now and I might take you back to your house." She watched him as he unbuttoned his pants. "And no biting. I want a simple blow job and nothing else. If you want to get off, you're on your own."

Fucking bastard. But he did have a nice cock. As soon as he fisted himself a couple of times, she felt her pussy heat up. Man, what it would be like to have that thing in her. Pulling her skirt up over her bare pussy, she played with herself, hoping he'd want a piece of her. But all he did was push her head to his cock, and she took him in her mouth.

Bella didn't care for sucking a cock unless she was being eaten, too. Sex in general, as far as she was concerned, was only good for one thing, and that was getting something for nothing. She knew that men watched her walk and knew they wanted her, but she never gave it up without getting something in return. She supposed all women felt the same way.

His cock was thick but not really that impressive now that it was up close and personal. She swallowed him down once or twice, and he held her still while he fucked her. Bella slid her fingers into her pussy, this time needing the relief that only she could give herself. As soon as he came, filling her mouth and throat with his hot cum, she did as well. But it was less than satisfactory.

"Fuck me." He shook his head as he did his pants up. "Come on. I'm wet and I bet I could make you hard again."

He just finished dressing, then slid under the steering wheel. Bella felt her temper get the better of her. As soon as he had the car moving, she hit him with her fist. As she hit him a second, then a third time, he tried to control her and the car. But she had finally reached into her purse and pulled out her tire iron, and hit him several times while he tried to shield his face. Bella didn't care so long as he knew that the next time she wanted something he gave it to her. The bumpity-bump of the car hitting something had her turn to look out the front window.

She couldn't see for all the blood. Wiping the window enough so that she could see, Bella saw that they'd hit a tree. Getting out, she realized that the idiot had also hit a parked car that was making all kinds of racket. Moving away from the man and the car, she reached into her purse and pulled out her jacket to pull over her. It, too, had blood on it, but she doubted anyone would notice the blood for her good looks. Bella moved along the streets to her house, smiling that she was getting the notice she deserved.

But Hannah was a problem. Without Hannah's job, and her income, Bella couldn't do the things she wanted to do. Like her hair. Fluffing it now, she had worked really hard that morning to color out the gray she'd noticed with a Magic Marker. It had gotten on her fingers, too, but she felt she'd done a good job in hiding the old hair. She'd thought about cutting it out again, but that had been such a mess the last time that she looked for other ways to deal with it. Then there was the rent.

Sure, they only had to pay a little bit because of them being poor all the time, but it was hard to even make that right now. Bella had gone into Hannah's room to find her stash, knowing that she had one, but had only managed to fuck the room up and not find a damned thing. How she could live in that blank room was beyond her. Bella loved color and thought that anyone who didn't was stupid.

The landlord was at her door when she came around the corner. Bella stayed out of sight until he moved away. She noticed that he'd hung something on her door again, and decided that she was just going to pretend she didn't see it like she had yesterday. Where the hell was she supposed to find…? "Damn it."

The guy who had given her a ride would have had money in his wallet. Bella actually thought about going back to see, but figured that by now somebody would have seen the blood and wondered where it had come from. She got into her apartment without disturbing the note and sat on her couch.

"What to do? What to do?" There was no one she could borrow anything from either. All her friends she'd borrowed money from before had told her this time that they weren't going to lend her money until she paid them back what she already owed them. Bella had told them about the beating that her daughter had given her again, but that didn't fly with them either. Bella would have to have old Pete beat her a little again before her daughter's trial.

Getting up, she went to the kitchen and fussed over the flooring again. They'd made such a mess of her house when someone had called for the ambulance. Why they couldn't have put a sheet under Hannah when they made her bleed was beyond her. And the spray paint she'd tried to cover it with only peeled up and came off on the bottoms of her shoes. Now she had big blotches of naked floor and purple patches of paint to show for all her good tastes.

Bella heard someone at the door a little after five and nearly didn't answer it. But looking out the peep hole she opened the door to the big man. Christ, he looked good enough to eat. She posed herself against the open door and showed him her best coy look. The man looked her up and down and she knew she had him.

"You here for something you like?" He took a step back and she pouted prettily at him. "Ah, you're not leaving me here all ready, are you? I've been looking for a man like you for years. And here you stand."

"Mrs. Oliver?" She nodded at him, then winked. "I'm here representing Miss Hannah Oliver. I think she's your daughter."

"She is. And whatever she's done now, I had nothing to do with it. I can barely move the way she knocks me around. Why, just last week I had to defend myself against her or she'd have kilt me."

"You're saying she hit you?" Bella nodded and moved into a better position. The man noticed her then, and she pushed out her breasts so he could get a good look at them. "Our report says that you hit her, but there was no mention of her hitting you."

"I don't like to let people know that my only daughter hits me. She's got a brain problem, you know. And I just don't like to talk about it." She tried another position only to have him look at the file in his hand. Was nobody going to help her out today? A quick fuck with him and she'd hit him up for some dough. But it wasn't going to work if he didn't look at her. Finally, she lifted her breast up with her hands and moaned for him. That certainly got his attention.

"Mrs. Oliver, I don't know what you think you're going to accomplish with this…this display, but I'm not interested in whatever it is you're trying to give me."

"Give you?" She laughed. "I never give it away, Mister…what did you say your name was?" She smiled at him again, and he shook his head. "Surely you'll give me your name so I can have something to scream out when I come, won't you?"

"It's Mr. Moran. And I doubt very much you'll be shouting out my name." He handed her an envelope. "You've been served, Mrs. Oliver. You're to appear in court on Monday morning. Good day."

He was gone before she could say anything to him, and by the time she did find her tongue, he was out of the parking lot. While she was standing there trying to think what to do now, her landlord came around the corner and pushed his way into her place.

"There's standards about paying on time, Bella. And as of right now, you're over six months behind in your rent. I've been okay with your daughter paying a little at a time but, well, you hurt her, and there won't be no more payments. Even small ones. Either pay up or I'm well within my rights to have you evicted." Bella wanted to stomp her foot and scream at her daughter, but she wasn't there and he was.

"Can I give you a down payment?" Wiggling her brows at him, she pulled off her blouse. Her bra barely hid anything, and she was glad now she'd taken the time to slip her jacket off and put on her silky pajamas. "I have a lovely bed upstairs. I bet we can come to some kind of arrangement."

"No, and hell no. I wouldn't touch you if…man, you have got to be kidding. Fuck you? Christ, lady, I wouldn't let my dog fuck you if I had one." He pulled out his cell phone and took two pictures before he backed out of her home. She stood there, stunned, while he called the police.

Bella shut the front door on him and tried to think. In this neighborhood she probably had like fifteen minutes to get gone. Grabbing up her purse, she went to the bathroom and slipped out the window. She'd done it before, and this time she didn't even cut her leg when she crawled out the broken window. By the time she heard the sirens screaming their arrival to her part of the world, Bella already had a nice little cozy place to stay in one of the many abandoned buildings not far from where she lived.

"Damn it, Hannah. This is all your fault." Bella had to get to her daughter and make her get a job. If she'd just kept her mouth shut and did what she'd told her, none of this would be happening. "I'll go back to that place tomorrow and have her released. She'll be so grateful that she'll get a job right away and help her mother out. It's the least she can do after I've put up with her all these years."

CHAPTER 7

Misha watched the man he'd been trailing for nearly three days with a kind of respect. He was good, he'd give him that. But Misha and his brothers were better. When he slipped into his car, the one that had the tracking device on it, he moved out of his hiding place to follow him. It was nearly over.

It had taken him longer to figure this one out than it had in a long time. Even Rider, who was usually very good at looking at a file and saying what was going on within minutes, was stumped. It finally took another death before they got a clue. And that was when Andrew stumbled onto a small stain on the floor of the second victim's apartment.

The man was going down today. Misha stopped by a shop window to look in when the man's car pulled to the sidewalk in the reflection. It was a woman's kind of shop, and he had a moment looking at one of the little nighties to wonder if Hannah would like it. But he turned from it when he heard something behind him. The man, Terry Barnshaw, was talking to a woman about where to grab some lunch.

"You could join me." Misha watched her shake her head no in the reflection of the glass. "Ah, come on. You've been very helpful, and I'd like to repay your kindness."

"No thanks." She started away but turned back. "You're new around here, aren't you? I guess…is that your car?"

Barnshaw glanced at the stolen car and nodded. The woman looked at it again before she moved on. Barnshaw leaned against the car and watched her. Misha turned to move down to the next shop when his mom touched his mind.

I just got a call from the judge. Do you have time to listen? He told her he did, and he held his breath waiting for the news. *She's been declared fit and will be released on Friday. He said there was no reason for her to stay in the hospital over the weekend when he'd already come to his decision. I was going to pick her up if you can't make it in the morning.*

I don't think we'll be finished here by then. He realized that he was sort of nervous now that she was going to be living with him. *Have you spoken to her? At all?*

I'm going over to talk to her today. She's been notified as well, he told me, and her mother, too. There were some issues with her, but nothing that they'd tell me about. Misha knew what they were; she was listed as a person of interest in the death of a man who had been bludgeoned to death. *Is there anything you need for me to tell her?*

I can't…I don't think so. I talked to her last night on the phone and she said that she was doing fine. The entire conversation had left him feeling like he'd been talking to himself. She'd answer his questions, but that was all. The one time she did speak first, it was to have him tell Carter thanks, and that was it. *We should be home in a couple of days. This is about to wrap up here.*

After he and his mom closed the connection, Misha moved through his part of the plan without thinking about what he was doing. Hannah was his mate and there was little to nothing he could do about it. And he'd realized when he hung up with her last night that he really wasn't sure he wanted to do anything about it. She was quiet, but he was sure that had more to do with her not knowing him rather than her being standoffish. Misha wasn't thrilled about her and Carter getting along so well, but that was simply because he'd been there for her more than Misha had been able to. Misha was going to try and do something about that when he got back.

He didn't want her to get the wrong idea about their relationship. There was never going to be anything between them, but they could be friends, he supposed. He'd heard Carter talking to Rider about her, how she could speak three languages and that she was a whiz at crossword puzzles. He'd also said that she was going to find a job as soon as she could.

And Carter leaving left a large hole in his heart. As soon as this business was over, he was going to move to the other side of the country. Misha's heart hurt each time he thought of his family pulling apart like this. He was taking on a whole new role as a mated leopard, and his entire family wasn't going to be there to support him.

He was being whiney, and he knew it. But things were just not...his mother was short with him, Rider barely spoke to him anymore, and even Andrew was avoiding him. The only time they seemed to agree on anything was when they were working. And sometimes even then it was a little—

I have a movement with the car. Where is it? Thomas sounded panicky, and Misha let a little of it wash over him. They had to get this man before it was too late for someone else. *Misha, are you there?*

The car is moving but just to another spot. I don't think he's doing more than just trolling. Does anyone know what the woman he'd spoken to is doing now? I'm worried he's not going to take no for an answer.

She's just standing in front of the drugstore. It looks like she's debating with herself. Rider laughed as he continued. *Probably trying to decide if she should go here or down to the local general store. Wait, she's moving toward me.*

There was silence for a bit from all of them, but Misha watched Barnshaw. When he moved his car again, Misha started to get a little nervous. What the hell was he doing? He told Thomas, who was closest to him, what was happening.

I see him. It's almost as if he's trying to find something closer to...where does that broad work? Someone must have answered him because Thomas spoke again. *Okay, this makes sense. She's more than likely on her break and he's trying to get closer to where she works. It'll make it easier for him to nab her if she's his intended.*

She fit the profile...tall, leggy, and blonde. Rider told them that he was following the woman. Misha asked him what was going on.

She knows the car. Or at least she thinks she does. I'm thinking...she had a long conversation with someone on the phone, and now I think she's on her way to confront him. If she does, then we're fucked. Misha started toward the car and the man. He saw the woman just as he was in front of the car.

"That's my cousin's car." Barnshaw stood up and Misha stilled. He told everyone to be on alert but to wait. "You might want to know that I've called the police, too. And they're coming here now."

Rider said that she hadn't, but the person on the other end might have. Barnshaw took several steps toward the woman and Misha had to stifle a laugh. She looked ready to beat his ass and he was pretty sure Barnshaw knew it.

"I don't know what you're talking about. This is my car." She was shaking her head. "It is. I think you should just leave me alone before you get yourself hurt."

"You think I'm afraid of you?" Her laugh was sarcastic and loud. "You are nothing but a two bit piece of shit. Come on, big boy, try me."

Misha, what the hell is she doing? He told Rider he didn't know, but it was making Barnshaw nervous and nervous people made mistakes. *Watch them.*

I am. The woman moved closer to Barnshaw while reaching into her large purse. When she pulled out a can of something, Misha started forward, only to come up short when she pulled a gun out, too. *Christ.*

"You're fucking nuts." She shrugged at Barnshaw, then fired at his feet. He dropped so quickly that Misha was impressed a man his size could move so fast. "I'm going to get you, bitch, see if I don't. You're just going to be another notch in my work area."

"You think so." Misha watched Rider move up behind the woman as he made his way to the man. As soon as he was within a couple of feet of the car, he smelled it. Blood. Then he saw the gun in the back of Barnshaw's pants. He told them what he'd found.

I think he has a body in the car. Rider took off running and lifted the woman off the ground just as Misha moved to grab the man who had pulled his own gun. The shots fired were fast and loud, and Misha had a moment of panic when he felt something tear into his shoulder. As he took

Barnshaw to the ground, Rider was pressing the woman against the building closest to them. It was over that fast.

They were waiting on someone to open the trunk. Misha would have already opened it, but since they weren't arresting him for that just yet, the police had to take over. All they had him on now was a gun charge. The woman, who was a retired cop herself, was being charged as well. Firing a weapon within the city limits was a hefty offense.

When the trunk was finally opened, three younger cops backed away from it. The smell alone was enough to make even a seasoned officer back off. But this was…the two women had been brutally beaten, almost to the point where it was going to be hard to identify them.

Misha was standing near one of the officers who had arrived first when all of a sudden he felt lightheaded and slightly sick to his stomach. He heard Thomas cursing and then Carter, but Misha was having a hard enough time just trying to focus on sliding to the ground. It wasn't until Rider shook him that he could hear.

"You've been shot, you stupid cock sucker." Misha thought his anger was funny and laughed. "You moron, why the hell didn't you say something?"

"Something?" Rider growled low and told him to shut the fuck up. "I think I need to lie down."

"You're on the fucking ground. It's small wonder that you're even…why the fuck didn't you say something?"

Misha thought about telling him again, but his head was suddenly pounding. He tried to sit up, but he couldn't seem to do it. When Carter came into his sight, Misha grabbed him.

"Don't leave me. Please, don't leave me." Carter nodded. "Never leave me. I need you with me. Please. I'm going to fuck this up and you have to help me."

"You're a prick, do you know that?" Misha nodded. "I'll stay until you get things settled. Not that I—"

Everything went black.

~~~

Han didn't know what to do with herself. The house was really nice, but it wasn't hers. Well, she supposed it was sort of hers. She did have a nice room with a bed, but the rest of the house was…it was sort of empty.

There was a chair in the living room that pointed toward the television, which was the biggest one she'd ever seen. The dining room was so bright with all the windows that she found herself there the most. There wasn't a table, so she could get around with her wheelchair pretty easily in there, which helped. The kitchen was the only room that was complete. It even had a cook.

"Miss Oliver, would you like some lunch?" She looked up at the big man and nodded. "Very well. I have luncheon meat if you'd like, as well as a pot of soup for you. Beef barley and crusty bread if you'd rather have that."

"May I have soup and a small sandwich?" He beamed at her and nodded. As he moved out of the dining room to the kitchen, Han looked out the window again.

There were trees everywhere. And flowers. They were fading, of course, but they still had enough color in them to give her a clue as to what might be there in the spring and summer. The last fall colors of the trees had her wishing she could paint, but she knew that even if she were very good, which she wasn't, she'd never be able to do them justice. The colors were just too beautiful. When Mr. Jackson called her to lunch, she moved into the big kitchen with him.

"Miss, there will be two more women coming by today for you to see about. I know that you don't like doing it, so perhaps it would help if I sat with you this time." Han flushed when she thought of the first woman she'd been asked to interview for house maid. "I have some experience in this field."

"She was…scary." Mr. Jackson nodded and grinned. "I had no idea…I've only seen Mr. Lanning a couple of times, but she knew things that…wow. Where on earth did she learn this stuff?"

"I believe she made most of that up. And you did very well with her, I think. Mr. Lanning would be quite proud of you for your quick thinking." Han doubted that. Maybe he'd want the other woman to work for him. She certainly made it clear as to what she wanted to do for him. "The agency that sent her along is most unhappy with the error. I don't think we'll get that sort of applicant again."

Han had confessed to Mr. Jackson that she had no idea what a house maid was to do. He'd sat her down and told her what would be expected of the woman they hired and what she wasn't to do. Giving the master of the house a morning blow job was not a part of her job description.

The interview had started out oddly. Even with her lack of experience, she knew that when dressing for a job interview, one didn't wear clothes that looked to be painted on and enough make up that a shower would be needed to wash it all off. The woman had reminded Han of her mother, and she'd taken an instant dislike to her. The interview went from bad to worse until Han had called for Mr. Jackson.

"I'd very much like for you to help Miss Crawford out, please." He looked at the woman with his eyes bugging out, then nodded at her. "She's overstayed her welcome."

"Where is the man of the house? I'm betting that while you're all laid up, he'll want a real woman in his bed. A morning woody to take care of with a quick blow job will be just the thing he'll love." Mr. Jackson rolled his sleeves up and moved toward the woman. "If you'd like, I could demonstrate on you how it would feel."

Mr. Jackson had picked up the woman and literally shoved her out of the house. She was cursing the entire time. When he came back to her, Han could see he was embarrassed more than she was.

"That was...I have...what did you...? Good Christ." Han had burst out laughing. When he joined her a few seconds later, they sat in the living room for a long while before he looked at her. "I have been told that you were hurt pretty badly by your mother. You are healing nicely if you don't mind me saying so."

"Most of the swelling has gone down, and my back is getting better, too. I can sit for a while without feeling all stiff." He nodded and sat up as she continued. "I'm not sure what I'm doing here. I know that I'm Mr. Lanning's mate, but he doesn't want me in his life."

Han didn't know why she'd told him that. She'd not even told Carter and he was her only friend. But Mr. Jackson told her she was going to be fine, and Han nodded. She was at a loss as to what do to.

The phone started ringing just as she was finishing her soup. She could tell immediately that something had happened. She was sure it was her mother and that she was coming for her, but when Mr. Jackson sat down after hanging up, she was worried for the Lanning men.

"Mr. Lanning...Misha Lanning has been shot." Before she could ask him if he was all right, he continued. "He's lost a great deal of blood, as he was shot very near to his heart. His brothers are with him, and Mrs. Lanning said she would come here for you if you wished to go with her to see him."

Did she? She didn't even know the man. But he was taking care of her, so she had no idea what to do. Before she could voice her concerns about how she was supposed to get anywhere in a wheelchair, Mrs. Lanning came into the house.

"I'm sorry, my dear, I should have called you first thing, but I'm not…I should have called you. Rider said he tried to call but you have no working number. Do you not have a cell phone?" Han shook her head, and Mrs. Lanning nodded. "I thought not. I'll make sure one of them takes care of that today. And Rider didn't have this number. I only just remembered I had it. Do you want to go?"

"How would…? I'm still in this thing. It would be hard for you to take me in your car." Mrs. Lanning was shaking her head, and Han found herself slightly disappointed that she'd not be able to go. "Thank you for asking me, however."

"Oh, honey, I meant to say, we're not driving. The plane is here waiting on us. I'll just have Jackson here take us over in the car and you'll be just fine." Han looked at Mr. Jackson, who winked at her. "We'll just get what we need there. I have it on good authority that he's doing better but a little cranky. Seeing how well you're doing will cheer him up."

Han doubted that. The man seemed to go out of his way to avoid her. She'd been doing the same, but the rules he'd given her stated that she was not to interfere in his life. Since she'd not seen him but only talked to him when he called, that was working out just fine.

They were being driven to the airport in a matter of minutes. Han had packed what little clothing she had, thanks to Carter getting her things and her money from her mother's house, but she still had to find a job soon. Money wasn't going to last long even if she didn't have to pay rent.

The trip was wonderful. Han had never been in a plane before, and when the man lifted her up and put her on the large couch she nearly hugged him to her. This was the most exciting thing she'd ever done. Mrs. Lanning sat across from her.

"May I ask you a favor?" Han thought that she'd do anything for this woman, even if she asked her to stay away from her. "I'd like for you to call me Maribel."

"That's your first name." She nodded and Han flushed. "I'm sorry. I didn't mean to sound stupid. I just never...why, if you don't mind me asking?"

"Well, I suppose it has to do with the fact that you're Misha's mate and we'll be spending a good deal of time together. But more than that, I like you a great deal, and Mrs. Lanning is so formal." Han nodded as Maribel continued. "You're not happy here, are you, my dear?"

"I'm not unhappy." Han wasn't sure she should tell this woman what she really felt, but Carter said that she'd understand. "He doesn't like me. I'm not sure what he wants with me hanging around his house, but he doesn't want me. Not even in his bed."

"I'm sure that he'll get over that." Han wasn't so sure and said that. "Misha was my confidante when his father was around. I might have...no, I did tell him things that I shouldn't have. His father didn't want us, and he made no bones about it. And Misha's heart is...it's broken, I suppose. And he's closed it off. Do you want him to love you?"

"No." Han watched the hurt on Maribel's face. "I don't want anyone to love me. It's too…I guess I really don't know what love is, but I've seen enough people profess that they love someone only to have it crumble in their faces. Working in the public, I got to see all sorts of things that showed me that love is very one sided most of the time."

"Your mother did that to you." Han thought maybe she was right but didn't say anything. "I'd like for you to love us all. Especially Misha. He could use a good woman like you to love him. And you need someone to love you as well. You deserve it."

"I just want to be left alone. I know that sounds really horrible, but it's harder to be hurt when you're alone." A man offered her a drink and some cookies. When she reached for her bag to pay for a couple of cookies, he told her it was fine. "See? I have no idea how to act around decent people."

Han wanted to cry. She was embarrassed and felt like she was completely out of her element. And now her provider was hurt and she had no idea what she was supposed to do about it. When Maribel unbuckled and sat beside her, Han had an overwhelming urge to lay her head on her lap and sob.

"Misha has a great deal of money. Well, they all do thanks to some sound investments and being really good at their jobs. This is just a part of the perks you'll have as his mate. Someone should have told you this before now, but if you never worked again, you'd have more than enough of everything you want."

"I don't want his money." Maribel nodded. "I'm going to make my own money as soon as I can. I don't want…I've only agreed to this whole thing because Carter said he'd go rogue if I didn't."

"He might…he very well might, but that's no reason for you to suffer if you don't want to. Being in a relationship is hard enough, having low expectations is only going to make it harder for both of you." Han wasn't planning to make anything hard on anyone and told Maribel that. "And if you fall in love with him? What will you do then? What about children?"

"He doesn't want children, he told me. Which I guess is fine with me as I have no idea what to do with them anyway. As for falling in love with him, it's doubtful that will happen, as he's told me that he'd rather I never bothered him and continued doing whatever it was I wanted so long as I didn't embarrass him or his family."

"I see." Han had a feeling she'd hurt Maribel somehow, but didn't know what to do about it. But the pilot told them to fasten their belts; they would be landing soon. When Maribel moved to her seat again, Han could feel the distance, and it was a great deal further than the few feet between them.

CHAPTER 8

Misha opened his eyes and tried to bring things into focus. He could make out shapes but not what they were. When the person in front of him moved, he knew who it was immediately. What the hell was Hannah doing in his room sleeping in his chair?

"Don't." He turned his head at his mother's voice spoken almost in his ear. "I have no idea what you're thinking right now, but if you make her cry again, I'm going to take you to the woodshed."

"I didn't make her cry. What is she…what are either of you doing in my room?" He looked around the room again, keeping his voice low, as he realized where he was. "I was shot."

"You were. And the next time this happens to you, I want you to know that I'm not coming to you again. You're a very mean man when you're hurting." Misha had no idea what his mom meant but looked at Hannah again. He could see now that she was sleeping fitfully, and he also could see the tear stains on her cheeks.

"What did I say to her?" He never took his eyes off her as he spoke to his mom. "She's beautiful."

His mom huffed at him, and he turned to look at her. She looked exhausted, and she'd been crying as well. When he reached up and touched his thumb to her cheek, she pulled his hand to her and hugged it. He looked around the room with better eyes.

"I'm in the hospital again." She smacked him in the chest before sitting down. He was careful when he rolled over because the pain had just made itself known to him. "How long have I been here this time?"

"Two days. We got here the day you were shot and she's not left your side. Even when you were mean to her." Misha looked over at Hannah again and marveled at the difference a week could make. "You told her that she was in your way and that you wished you'd never met her. How could you, Misha?"

He had no idea. "I wasn't thinking clearly, I suppose. What was she doing when I said it? I mean, I didn't mean to hurt her."

"You didn't." He looked over at Hannah when she spoke. When her chair backed up, he was sure she was leaving and asked her to stay. "I have to go to the bathroom. And you should visit with your family."

She was out the door before he could say anything. Looking at his mom, Misha wasn't sure what to say about her look either. His mom was hurt, and Misha felt terrible about it.

"She's my family, too." His mom nodded but didn't speak. "I don't know what to do with her."

"She said the same thing about you. I told you this was a mistake. I wish…neither of you are going to make it if one of you doesn't try at least a little. Phillip said you called for her for the entire time you were being brought here. Then when she saw you, you told her to get away from you and to leave you in peace."

"I've been having dreams…nightmares about her. Not her really, but nightmares that she's hurt and I can't get to her. I think her mother is involved some, but I can't keep her safe." Misha leaned back on the bed. "The gunshot. It was silver? That's why I couldn't shift."

"Rider said you were all right for a little while and he figured you were waiting to get somewhere you could shift. Then you started to fall, and he knew that you'd been shot with silver. By the time they'd removed it from your body, you'd lost a great deal of blood and shifting wasn't possible. I'm sick of you being hurt all the time, Misha. You need to take better care of yourself."

All he could think about was how he'd hurt Hannah.

"Do you think you could go find her for me? I should apologize to her. I don't want her to be upset." His mom looked at him hard. He wasn't sure, but he had a feeling she was looking deep into his heart. There was nothing there; even he knew that.

She stood up without saying anything and left him. Misha moved around in the bed so that he could see her when she first came in. But he wasn't prepared for her when she finally did. This time his vision was much clearer, and he realized she wasn't just beautiful, she was gorgeous.

"I'm sorry I hurt you." She just shook her head and looked out the window. He wanted her to come closer but wasn't really sure why. The need to touch her made his cat pulse along his skin. "Could you come closer to me? I have to…my cat needs to touch you."

"You're going turn into a cat?" Her voice was high, and she cleared her throat before she continued. He might have thought it was funny if he didn't really want to shift and take her to the floor. "I guess you could do anything you want, and shifting or whatever it's called is something I'll need to get used to."

She didn't move and he asked her again to come closer. As she moved forward, Misha sat up on the bed and threw his legs over the side. He was lightheaded, but it was from his need to be with her rather than the loss of blood.

"What are you going to do?" He stood up when she was within touching distance and put his hand on hers. "Mr. Lanning, you don't think you should stay in bed?"

The thought of staying in bed, his bed with her beneath him, nearly took his breath away. Lifting her chin up so that he could look into her eyes, Misha felt his cock stretch and thicken. He leaned down to her slowly.

"I'm Misha. Say it please. I want to hear you say my name." Her breathless reply had him grinning. "Not Mr. Lanning. Misha. Say it, Hannah. Say my name so I can kiss you properly."

"I don't know how. Know how to kiss at all." He brushed his mouth over hers, happy with her confession. "You should stop now."

He ran his tongue over her lips and watched as she ran her own over her lips, as if she were tasting him there. With a small groan, he took her lower lip into his mouth and suckled it until she put her hand on his arm. Her breathless "Don't" made him want more.

The kiss, soft and gentle, only made him hungry for more of her. When she tightened her fingers on his arm, Misha cupped the back of her head and deepened the kiss. She opened her mouth under his, and Misha moaned again.

Her tongue shyly touched his, and her lips opened more when he rolled his tongue over hers. He wanted to pull her up, wrap her around him, but knew, in the back of his mind, that she was injured and lifting her would be painful. But Christ, he wanted her. When he raised his head from hers for just a second, she licked her lips and stared at him.

"I wish you weren't in pain." She nodded. "I could lay you out on this bed and bury myself deep inside of you. It's what I want to do more than anything right now. My cock, it aches to take you."

"I don't...you said that you didn't really want me that way." He kissed her again, showing her with his mouth just how much he really wanted her. Finally, he lifted her up in his arms and carried her to the bed. "What are you going to do?"

"I don't know, but I have to...I have to do something." He moved his gown out of his way and fisted his naked cock. She watched him as he felt his balls tighten to his body. "Could you take off your blouse? I want to...I want to come all over you this way."

She started for the hem of her shirt, but his cat wasn't waiting. He snarled at him to take her, and Misha reached down and tore her shirt from her. The look on her face made him take her mouth again. The need there was more than he could hope for. When he lifted his head this time, she was panting, and he was as well.

"Undress. I won't take you this way, but I need to come on you. I need to be sure that no one else will touch you." She didn't say anything but worked at the clasps on her bra. Once she had it off, Misha laid her back on the bed and took her hard nipple into his mouth. Her fingers curling in his hair had him opening his mouth wider and sucking hard of as much flesh as he could take in.

Misha was hurting now. His cock was so full that he knew the moment he had her naked he was going to come. When she worked at the soft pants she had on, he stepped back and pulled them over her cast. She was naked now, and he could only stare. When she tried to cover herself with his sheet, he stopped her.

"No. Please don't. I want to…let me see you." She nodded but closed her eyes. Misha knew that she was a virgin and more than likely overwhelmed right now, but he couldn't stop from touching her. "Your pussy is calling to me. I want to drink from you. Could I taste you?"

He didn't wait for an answer but ran his fingers over her curls then into her heat. She was soaking wet, and he slid his finger into her. He took her juices to his mouth and sucked them dry. He needed more.

"I'd like to taste you, Hannah." He leaned down to bury his nose in her pussy and licked her from gate to clit. Nibbling on her hard little nubbin, he heard her moan, and he stood up again. "Christ, you're going to drive me insane."

Reaching blindly behind him, he pulled her chair to him. Sitting down, he rolled forward until he could put her thighs on either side of his head, careful of her cast. When she sat up and looked at him, he slowly leaned down to her and took her into his mouth. Misha knew for as long as he lived, the taste of her was going to haunt him.

Cupping her ass, he brought her to his mouth. The more he drank of her, the more her juices flowed from her, the more Misha wanted. Nipping at her clit again, he felt her stiffen as she cried out. Her climax only made him want to give her more.

"Please." Misha lifted his head from her when she came twice more. He loved having her come in his mouth and wanted more than anything to have her do it over and over. "Too much. It's too much."

He stood up then, and fisted his cock again. He had to mark her, had to spread his seed all over her heated body so that no one else would touch what was his. The moment she touched him however, wrapped her fingers around his cock, Misha knew that he had to be inside of her.

Lifting her cast-covered leg, he rested it on his shoulder. Misha slid just the crown of his cock in and out of her as she cupped her breast. Her moans, her heat, were making him insane with need and he slid deeper. She looked up at him as he touched her virginity.

"It's going to hurt when I enter you." Hannah put her hand over her mouth. "I'm sorry. So sorry."

Misha slammed forward and felt himself break past the barrier. He stilled his body over hers when she screamed. He'd hurt her, he'd really hurt her, and he was sorrier than he'd ever been for anything.

"Just let me...I can't move, baby. If you calm down a little, I'll be able to pull from you." She nodded but seemed to tighten around him. "Hannah, you're making me harder."

The next time she moved it was to roll her hips. Misha couldn't help but roll with her. Every time he moved, every single time her body seemed to wrap around him tighter, he slid his cock deeper until he was buried to the root. He leaned over her and took her mouth gently.

"I'm going to come inside of you. I'm going to mark you so that no other man will come near you. If they do, I'll kill them." She looked at him then, and Misha knew that she understood him. "I have to mark you, Hannah, and this is the only way."

She only stared up at him as he started to move. He tried to be easy on her, knowing that he was hurting her again, but he was so close. When he felt his balls begin to empty, his cock flooding her with his cum, he held her to him and nipped hard at her shoulder. When he tasted her blood again, he wanted to have her bite him, too, but she cried out again, and he felt it was from pain rather than from her release, and held her tightly as he emptied into her again.

~~~

Hannah wasn't sure what to do now that he'd finished. She was in a great deal of pain and not just physically. Her back hurt, as did her pussy, but it was her heart that felt as if he'd shattered her. But for such a large man, he was holding her like she was a fragile flower or something like a priceless artifact.

She wasn't even sure what she thought would happen now that he'd taken her. He'd told her all along that there would be nothing between them. And that sex, when he wanted it, was going to be simply a release for him and her if she chose. But to tell her that it was simply a ritual of his, while she had really been enjoying herself...well, she would have to be more careful in the future with sex.

"Are you all right?" She nodded and realized that he might not be able to see her the way he was laying, so she answered him. "I'm really sorry. I only meant to mark you so that no other—"

"You said that." He lifted his head and looked down at her. "Could you please help me back to my chair? This isn't very comfortable."

He helped her to sit up after he pulled free of her. The pain took her breath away, and she tried to not let him know, but he heard her, she supposed. But instead of putting her into the chair, he helped her to lay in the bed better and covered her nudity up with his sheet. As he sat in the chair, he held her hand until she nodded. A place she didn't want to be. Before she could tell him she'd rather just leave, he went to the little closet in his room and began pulling on his clothing. She turned away when he bent at the waist to pull on his pants.

"I didn't mean to take you that way. I'm sure I hurt you, but it won't hurt the next time." She turned to look at him, and he laughed. "You didn't think that would be the first and only time, did you?"

"Yes. I had hoped it would be." He frowned but said nothing as he pulled his shirt over his head. "I'd like to leave now, please. I should have left before now."

"First, you have no shirt to wear. Secondly, I'd like to talk to you about why you're upset. Did I hurt you that badly?" She shook her head. "Then why are you trying to get away from me?"

"I don't want to be with you, period, Mr. Lanning. I'm only here because I was told you'd go rogue if you didn't have me as your mate." He sat down and stared at her. "You don't love me. I don't love you. We're here because someone thought it would be funny for us to be together. You said yourself that we're not going to be a good match. And I think that's as good a reason as any to not have sex again."

"I want you again right now." She flushed hotly when he pulled the sheet off her body. "Right now I could take you, bury myself deep inside of you, and have you screaming out a release. Don't you want that?"

She did and she was pretty sure that he knew it. But all he did was pull the sheet over her and step back. When he left her, closing the door behind him, she let the tears fall. She wasn't even sure what she was crying for. When the door opened again, she wiped quickly at the tears and stared at Mrs. Lanning.

"He said that he hurt you." Hannah nodded. "And I'm not thinking it was just with him taking you, was it?"

"I'd like to leave here now." Maribel nodded and reached into a bag she had and handed her a pretty green blouse. "I'll make sure you get this back."

"I bought it for you. I knew you didn't have much in the way of clothing and I wanted you to have this." Hannah nodded and held the gift to her heart. "People aren't very good to you, are they? They've crapped on you for a very long time, and you just don't know how to act when someone is truly nice to you."

"My mother hated me but for the things I could give her. Rent money and things. Well, more often than not it would be for her clothing and hair and nails, but that's all. I've never had a boyfriend because as soon as someone started to show interest in me, she'd tell them what I was." Maribel asked her what she thought she was. "Insane."

"You're not insane, child. I thought Carter proved that to you." Hannah nodded. "I'm sorry he hurt you, Hannah. Truly I am."

"It doesn't matter anymore. We've made our lives what they are and little can be done about it now." Hannah knew the futility of trying for something better. "If you could give me a moment, I'd very much like to leave here. I would like a bath."

As soon as Maribel turned her back, Hannah slipped the blouse over her head. There were no tags on it so she had no idea how much it had cost, but she knew it was a good deal more than she'd ever paid for anything she had, as most of it had come second hand or more from friends of her mother or Goodwill. As she was helped into the wheelchair again, Hannah tried to think what she was supposed to do now.

The plane ride back was made mostly with Misha talking to his brothers. When he tried to get her to talk to him, she pleaded a headache, which wasn't a lie. Everything about her hurt right now, especially her heart. When they got to the house, she was lifted from the back of the limo by Misha and carried into the house.

She could see a car in the drive but had no idea whose it was, nor did she care. Moving slowly to the room she'd taken when she got there, she was surprised to hear her name. Turning, she looked at Misha.

"I'm sorry." She nodded but said nothing. "I don't know what to do about you. I've never wanted a mate and now that I have one, I have no idea what to do with you."

A million things came to mind, but she didn't voice any of them. At the top of the list was to let her go. But she didn't have anywhere to go if he did, and living with her mother after what she'd done to her was out of the question. When he sat down on the chair, she didn't move but did look toward her room.

"I'd like to talk to you. I have…I want to tell you something I've never told anyone before." She asked him why. "I don't know. But after the way I treated you, I suppose I feel as if I owe you something."

"You mean like a prostitute." He looked shocked. "I know how it works, Mr. Lanning. A man makes all sorts of promises to a woman. Then, when it comes to sex, things get all screwed up. I don't want anything from you. I'm well aware of what my duty is to you."

"Duty?" She nodded, and he leaned back in the chair and chuckled. "Do you have any idea how I'm…? No, you don't. How could you when all I've done is shove you away? Christ, you must really hate me."

"I don't have any feelings for you one way or the other. And I'd like to keep it that way." She felt her heart take an unexpected twist and tried to ignore it. "Loving people is painful, as you've said to me before. Not in those words, but it was the same thing. I don't have anything in my chest that will let me love anyone. It's too…it hurts too much."

"You can't ever love me." She shook her head, and her heart twisted harder until she couldn't breathe around the pain. "I'm sorry for that then. Because as much as I wanted to keep you out of my heart, you've managed to seep in."

"You haven't known me long enough to love me, Mr. Lanning. We've only just become acquainted." He stood up and began pacing the room, and she watched him.

She could see him as a large cat, sleek and huge. And that wasn't just his cat. The man himself was huge, too. And though she knew very little of men, Han knew that he would be considered ripped. His muscles had muscles, and she wondered if he could lift large cars without breaking a sweat. He was wearing a shirt now, but she'd felt them ripple beneath her fingers when she'd held him, felt them tighten when he'd come. The tightly trimmed beard had burned against her breast when he'd suckled at her, and when she'd curled her fingers into his hair, all she could think about was how his fur would feel when or if she ever got to feel it. The man reeked of sex and sex appeal.

But it was his eyes that mesmerized her the most. They were the most beautiful shade of blue she'd ever seen, crystalized and clear. She thought if she ever saw the ocean, it would pale in comparison. And when he looked at her, sometimes she had a feeling that he could see into her very soul, deeper maybe.

When he turned to her, she wanted to back from him, but she wasn't sure she could. He had trapped her there as if he'd held her with his hands. Flushing slightly when he smiled, she did move back from him.

"I've made a terrible mistake. I hurt you. I know that…all of this is my fault, but I'd very much like to make it up to you. Hannah, we're going to be spending the rest of our lives together, and I don't want you to hate me." She started to tell him she didn't hate him when he continued. "I'm going to do everything in my power to have you fall in love with me. I'm going to show you how much love can do for you. And I'll be learning that with you. If you don't, then it's the very least that I deserve. But trust me when I tell you, I have fallen in love with you."

"I don't want you to love me. I'm not…I just don't want it." He pulled her out of the chair and to his body. The kiss he gave her was breathtaking and she held onto him, afraid that he'd do more than kiss her…or worse yet, push her away. When he lifted his head but held her to him still, she looked up at his smiling face.

"Christ, you're beautiful." She shook her head. "You are. And you're all mine. Forever. As of right now, I'm going to prove to you and to myself that I can love you more than either of us have ever been loved."

"No one loves me." He kissed her again and picked her up in his arms. "You have to put me down. I will need my chair later."

"I'm going to give you a bath. I'm betting that after me taking you so hard today, you're sore. If you'd let me lick you again, that would take the pain away." He wiggled his brows at her, and she shook her head. "Oh well. Maybe next time."

"I don't want you to give me a bath. I'm capable of giving myself a bath." She squeaked when he put her on the counter. "Mr. Lanning, you can't—"

"Misha." She stopped talking to watch him as he pulled his shirt over his head while the water splashed into the big tub. "My name is Misha. You're Hannah. Do you have a middle name?"

"Marie. And what do you think you're doing? You put your clothing back on right now." He just grinned at her as he pulled his pants off, leaving his boxers on. "Mr. Lanning, you have to—"

He pressed her back on the counter and moved between her legs. When he rocked into her, she moaned and grabbed his shoulders. She tried her best not to enjoy what he was doing, but when he cupped her ass in his large hands and pulled her to his cock, she moaned again.

"Could you call me Misha? Scream out my name while I make you come? Say my name while I bury my cock deep into your heat? While your body ripples around mine when you come?" She felt her body expanding at his words, her nipples tightening under the silken blouse, and her pussy thickening with need much like his cock was at her opening. "Say it, Hannah Marie; say my name and I'll make you come."

He rocked harder and faster. Her legs lifted up on their own, and she wrapped them around him as he leaned her back on the counter. When he started to open her blouse, she stopped him with her hands and unbuttoned it for him. She didn't want him tearing her first gift.

"So lovely. Your breasts are so lovely that I could suckle them all day and never get enough." He took her nipple into his mouth and chewed gently on the tip. "Do you like this? I can smell that you do, but tell me."

"Yes." She did, too, and curled her fingers into his hair to bring him back to her. "I don't want this."

He laughed, lifted her up, and pressed her to the wall. His cock was rubbing her clit so hard that she felt her entire being readying for him. When he pulled her pants down, over her ass then the cast, she knew that he was going to enter her again, and she stiffened at the thought.

"I'm not going to hurt you. Relax for me." He moved his fingers down her body to her pussy and slid inside of her. "You're so wet. And hot. Christ, I don't know whether to eat you until I have my fill or slide deep inside of you and stay there."

"It'll hurt. You're too big." He moved his fingers, and she felt his cock then. It was so thick and hard that she tried to pull back. "Don't hurt me."

"Come for me." He pinched her clit, and she screamed. It was overwhelming and unbelievably amazing. When he filled her, his cock moving inside of her, she could only feel how he fit her and looked at him.

"You're wrapped around me so tightly." He moved as he held her ass over him. "Come for me, Hannah. Come hard and let me bite you again."

Her body responded to his command. She not only came, her body soaring up over an incredible peak, but it fell back down twice more before she could catch her breath. He licked her shoulder, and Hannah knew that he was going to bite her again. Her own need to bite him reared up, and she sank her teeth into him before she could think that it was a bad idea.

He came then, crying out her name as he pounded into her. Hannah tasted his blood, and felt it run down the back of her throat as he sank his teeth into her. As soon as she screamed, he pulled her tighter and tore at her flesh. Hannah felt her world center then, her mind snap into a different place, and her heart beat harder in her chest. Then as she came again, crying out his name this time, she knew that she was going to faint. Her body simply slipped away as she came a fourth, then a fifth time.

CHAPTER 9

"Found it." Bella crawled out from under the bed and sat on the floor. She'd destroyed Han's room looking for the information, and now she had it. The envelope also had the key and the information to the post office box as well. "Damned kid. How the hell was I supposed to find it if you hid it like that?"

She'd had to crawl into the broken bathroom window to get into the apartment. Bella didn't mind that so much except that someone had been there before her. The entire house was emptied of nearly every piece of her good stuff. The only thing that they didn't bother was Hannah's things. Her room had been as nasty cleaned up as ever.

"Or it was." Smiling, Bella got up and moved out of the trashed room, thinking she'd take a nice long shower and change into one of her dresses before going to the store. She knew the guy down there would give her cash for the food money on the card. She might be able to get her nails done, too, if she gave him a little extra.

She'd never understood the child. Hannah hadn't just been a disappointment to her but had also been a stick in the mud when it came to having fun. Even before the thing with her being committed, she'd been sort of strange to her.

If she had to do it over again, Bella might have just left her with her dead mother.

Always wanting to read instead of watching Bella's programs with her like a good child should have, Han had been good in school and never had to have any calls from the teacher. Which, she supposed, was good, but Bella wanted her to be bad, and to be sexy like her. Even her lack of style had been a mystery to her. She preferred things to be orderly and white rather than colorful and eclectic. Bella liked color and a great deal of it. Purple and pink were her favorites.

Bella was standing in her closet when she heard the door open. She knew the voice of the one man but not the other. Pulling the door closed behind her, Bella stood in the closet with her dress in her hands as the men moved about the rooms. It wasn't until they were in her room that she could actually understand what they were saying.

"...today, but that was a done deal even before all this. I liked the kid. Quiet and all, but that mother of hers…well, she wasn't anyone I'd want raising me."

"Hannah is in good hands now. We're going to be married in a few days. I'm glad that I found her. It's really too bad that the mother is such a piece of shit." Bella grabbed the door to open it and tear into the man. But his next words, chilling and delivered with such calmness, had her pause. "If I ever get the opportunity to meet her, I'm going to show her just what it's like to be beaten within an inch of her life." He sounded as if he were standing right in front of her.

"I heard that she beat that girl of hers up. I was off that day, or you can bet I would have been right there helping them find her. No cause for that. None at all. Hannah always made sure that she told me right up front when the rent was going to be late. She never said why, but she'd be wearing bruises when she'd tell me. I just knew that mother of hers had spent it all." The door closed again and the voices faded away. Bella stood there as still as she could for a long time. She had no idea why, but she thought the man knew she was hiding in there.

Shivering, she finished dressing when she heard the front door close, then went to put on her makeup. Bella took several steps back from the counter, enough to be plastered against the wall, when she saw what was laying there. Her shoe, the one she'd had on when she'd beaten Hannah that day, and a business card.

"Misha Lanning of Lanning Search and Rescue." She snorted and put the card back on the shoe. "What's he going to do, rescue me? I don't need nobodies recusing me. I've gots my shit together."

She was putting on the pretty black eyeliner when she thought of something else. She wondered, just for a moment, if her daughter was going to be better off than she was. When a person could afford a business card, especially one like this, maybe he had some money. She moved toward the kitchen again with only one eye finished and pulled out the phone book.

The ad was huge, almost the whole page. And there in the middle of it were six of the most beautiful men she'd ever laid eyes on. Right there at the front of the line of names was Misha. Bella smiled.

"Gotta love a man that is looking like that one. Maybe I'll just pay him a visit after all. He did leave me his calling card." Moving back to the bathroom, Bella paid extra care to the rest of her makeup. Going calling required that she looked her best, and something that Bella always prided herself on was looking her very best. Looking in the closet again, she pulled out her best dress. Not bothering with a bra or panties, she pulled the other dress off and slipped the fresh one over her head. Sex was all men thought about, and she knew she was the sexiest thing he'd ever see on high heels.

Bella moved back and forth in front of her mirrors and smiled at herself. "Damn, I look good."

Her dress was a pale blue and nearly see-through. If she pinched her nipples hard enough, a person could see them just fine. And her pussy, all clean shaven, was visible just an inch or two above the short skirt of the dress. With no back at all, it draped over her body like a wetsuit. She even thought the tat she'd gotten the other day looked fine peeking out on her thigh. She was as ready as she'd ever be to see her man.

"What would Hannah do with a man like that anyway? Stupid girl wouldn't know how to please a man. Hell, she's not even tried out any of mine when I was willing to share." Bella snorted again when she pulled out her nicest purse and stuffed her food card and keys in it. "Maybe I can get him to have me in some apartment when he gets bored with the little bitch, and I can show him what a real woman does for her man."

Bella shivered when she thought of what this man might have below his belt. She'd bet anything a man that big would have a cock that would make her enjoy sex. And him riding her? Damn, it was making her all wet just thinking about him. Bella stood at the front door, then hurried back to the bathroom. She'd almost forgot his token for her. The card was put in her purse with her other things, and she moved out the door.

The trip to the post office was done on foot. If her calculations were correct, she should have one of them government checks in the mail. She got her Social Security check sometime during the month and never used it much for paying bills. She was going to splurge this time and maybe get herself a nice new pair of shoes with some of it. But she needed to get it first.

The post office was busier than she remembered it being before. But then Bella rarely went there unless it was to get her check when her daughter couldn't. But it had been years since that had been a problem. Hannah knew better than to hold out on that one ever again.

Bella stood in front of the long rows of boxes. Some of them were huge, some not much bigger than what would hold an envelope. And she had no idea which one was hers. Staring at them for a long time, she tried to remember if Hannah had ever told her, but knew that she wouldn't have. Hannah liked her secrets. And even though Bella had set up the box, she had long since forgotten what the number was. She went to stand in the line to get some help.

People were staring at her. Twice she wanted to pull out her compact and see what it was. Maybe she had something in her teeth or a hair out of place, but she'd forgotten the compact on the counter. She smiled at one young man, and he backed from her so quickly that she laughed. Men were always blown away by her looks and her sexual appeal. When her turn came, she smiled at the person at the counter and told him what had happened. Or at least her version of what had happened.

"And I don't have any idea what has happened to my little girl. And for the life of me, the number isn't coming to my mind." She smiled her best watery smile at him, and he didn't even blink. Her first thought was she'd gotten a queer. Then he looked her over.

"Ma'am, you have to know your number before I can help you. Do you?" Bella shook her head, then sniffled again. "Then I'm afraid you're out of luck. Especially since you have no identification on you as well."

"But I needs my money. I gots to go and see the big man in the picture." She reached into her bag for his card again, but the man in front of her was telling the next person he could help them. "I'm not done here. I needs for you to open my mail thingy up and give me the check. It's the first of the month."

"It's the nineteen of the month. And as I've said, I can't help you without you having the number or any kind of identification. You'll need to move along or I'll have to call the police." She glared at him for several seconds until he picked up the phone. Bella wasn't stupid enough to think that the cops would be on her side, so she left. She supposed she should have thought of Hannah as making sure she was down on her luck. The kid had been nothing but trouble since that woman, child really, had squirted her out…however many years ago it had been. Damned girl.

The bus would only take her as far as downtown. They wouldn't take her directly to the address on the card, and she argued with the driver for five minutes before he, too, threatened her with the police. What the hell was wrong with people nowadays? Didn't anyone ever want to do something because it was nice?

Bella walked the last five blocks and was pissed off by the time she got to the big building. Then looking at the door, she saw that it said that they didn't open until noon. The fucking bastard could have told her that when he'd left her his card. She looked around for something to tell her the time and stopped a person.

"It's gone five-thirty. They won't be back in until tomorrow." She looked at the times again and wasn't surprised to see that they worked until five. Mother fuck, now what the hell was she supposed to do?

Looking for an abandoned building, Bella found one about five blocks from the office. She was going to have to have him give her something nice for all the trouble she'd been through to get to him. Bella thought of all the really nice things she'd be getting and smiled.

Taking off her dress so it wouldn't get mussed, she lay down on the newspapers that she'd gathered up from around the rooms. Too bad there wasn't a nice bed, but she realized that beggars couldn't be begging. "Or something like that."

She was sound asleep within minutes and thinking about how much she was going to enjoy going down on her big Misha. And maybe if her daughter was nice to her, she'd let her join her so she could learn a few things from dear old Mom. Bella was going to be set for life.

~~~

Misha knew that she was going to be sore, incredibly so, but he couldn't help but smile every time he thought of how she'd said his name when she'd had her climax last night. He knew that it wasn't much, but to him, it was as if she'd handed him the world. He watched her sleep on the little bed and tried to think how he could get her to sleep with him every night for the rest of his life. Well, not sleep, but make love. He'd never even made love to her in a bed yet, and he could see them together in his bed.

Going to the bathroom, he emptied the tub and started to refill it. She would need a warm bath more than ever now. As it filled, he thought of the one in his room and hoped that soon he'd be able to get into it with her. Going back into the bedroom, he found her awake.

"You should sit in some warm water for a while." She nodded, and he could see her blush. For whatever reason, that made him smile as well. "I'll help you. I know you can't get your casts wet, so I've put a stool in the tub to hold it up for you."

"I can manage." He heard her brisk tone but knew it was more due to embarrassment than anger. She'd get used to him soon enough. When she winced, he moved to the bed to help her up. And that's when he saw her back. They'd torn open some of the wounds.

"I should have remembered these and taken better care with you." Instead of picking her up, he had her lay on her stomach while he looked at them. "I'm sorry, baby. I should have done something about these sooner. Let me heal them."

"How?" Instead of answering her, he simply licked a path along the one still bleeding. She cried out but he knew it wasn't from pain. Her arousal hit him like she'd slapped him with it. "Stop that. It's not healthy."

"I can't catch anything even if you had something. Lie still. I need to do this for you." He wanted to roll her over and taste her breasts this way, but he knew she had to be hurting more than she was showing him. Besides, he had to get to work today. He'd been taking too much time off as it was.

"I can do this." He wanted to swat her ass but just resisted the urge. "I'm...will you just stop that?"

He'd licked them all closed but the one. It was just at the curve of her ass and he'd been trying his level best to avoid it. It was simply too tempting not to lift her up and take her like that. Instead, he ran his tongue over her and nearly gave in to his temptation when she moaned.

"They shouldn't give you any more trouble." She turned over and stared at him as he backed from the bed. "I'd like to have you sleep in my room from now on."

"No." He'd figured that would be her answer and nodded. She looked around the room and not at him before she continued. "You said that I'd be safe here and that you'd not want me in your bed much. I was counting on that."

Misha tried not to let her words anger him, and he took a deep breath before he spoke. "I like making love to you."

"We're not making love. We don't love each other. It's just…it's just sex." He laughed, and she glared at him. "You don't love me. Admit it. You're just saying that because you think it's what I want to hear."

"No. I love you. I didn't think it was possible, but I do." She didn't say anything, but he could tell she was upset. Instead of upsetting her more, he leaned down and kissed her. Before he could lift his head, however, he cupped the back of her head and deepened the kiss.

Backing away from the bed before he joined her there, he smiled at her confused look. It was only fair. He thought that she was just as confused as he was about this. "I have to go into the office today. But I should be back around six. If I have to change that, I'll let you know. Okay? Oh, and there is water running in the bathtub for you. You should try to sit in it for a little while. If you want, I can heal it like I did your back. I'm sure that we'll enjoy that a great deal more."

"Why are you doing this to us? Why don't you…? We had rules set down. You don't want to…there is no way that you can love me." He started to ask her why when she started crying. "I'm not a baby, but you're driving me insane. I don't know what to do with you."

"I don't either, honey."

Leaving the room, he went downstairs to find his cook and longtime friend making bread. The man never ceased to amaze him with his cooking. He sat down and tried to think of a single reason why he shouldn't go into work today.

"You're going." He looked up at Jackson. "You've mated with her; bonded, too. Give her a break. You can be a mite overwhelming when you're like this."

"Like what?" Jackson handed him a warm scone and a glass of juice. "What do you mean, when I'm like this?"

"You're all hard-assed and mean when you want to be, but you're like...well, day old cereal when you're around her. Have you figured out you're in love with her yet?" Misha nodded. "Good. But don't expect her to be quick about it. She's not used to people loving her, and she don't know how to love you back. She will, but she's just not knowing how yet."

"Her mother did that to her." Jackson nodded but didn't speak. "I didn't want to love her. I didn't even want a mate. But now that I have her...is it possible for a person to fall so much in love only after a few weeks?"

"For us, it's a necessity. Sort of like our wild counterpart. We find a mate and start having little ones to repopulate the world. She's a nice girl, but she's a little on the...I was going to say shy, but I don't think that's it. I think she's more not quite ready."

"Ready?" Jackson nodded and didn't answer. "She seems like she's been beaten up, and I don't mean just physically. Do you think she'll get over that someday?"

"I do. And when she does, I'd suggest you shut up and pay attention to her. She's going to blow you and the other Lanning men right out of the water." Jackson laughed hard as he put the bread in the loaf pans. "Yes, sir, she's going to knock you on your ass so hard you aren't going to know what hit you."

Misha left the house a few minutes later, having been nearly thrown from the kitchen by Jackson. He thought about Hannah all the way to work, and when he pulled into the lot behind their building, he nearly turned and went back to be with her. Getting out before he did that, he was at his desk starting up his computer when Andrew came in and sat down.

"There's...something here to see you." His brother looked like he might be ill. Before he could ask him if he was sick, he continued. "I was going to say someone was here to see you, but I'm not sure that what's out there is human. Not like us inhuman, but simply...Christ. You have a visitor."

"Who is it?" Misha leaned back in his chair while Andrew seemed to try and think what to say. It was funny, and Misha laughed at him. "What is it then?"

"She hit on me." Andrew shivered and closed his eyes. "If I ever get that desperate, I want you to kill me. I wouldn't touch that if my very life...I'm not sure...Christ."

"You said that." Misha had a feeling he knew who it was, and even though he had no idea what she looked like, he did know her scent. "Is it by any chance Bella Oliver?"

Andrew nodded, then looked at him sharply. "That's Han's mother? Mother fuck, she must be adopted. That thing out there no way gave birth to that vision that you're mated to. Seriously?"

"I believe so. I've never met her, but I left her my card yesterday when I went by Hannah's house to see if there was anything she'd need from there. And there wasn't. At all." He knew that Carter had gone there as well and had gotten an envelope for Hannah, but not what else he might have picked up. As far as Misha was concerned, there was nothing there that Hannah would ever need again. "Did she say what she wanted?"

Andrew shivered again and nodded. "Us. Particularly you. And I don't think she just meant to talk to you either. I think she wants you." He stood up and shook all over. He was moving toward the door when Misha said his name.

"I need you to stay." Andrew started to argue, but Misha laughed. "I need someone to stay here and make sure that she doesn't rape me. You never know what she might say happened if she doesn't get whatever it is she wants."

"I don't think she'll care if you had an entire squad of men in here. She looks like she's one determined woman." He looked at the door as if he might bolt. "I'll get the others to come in as well. There is no reason why you should have all the...Christ, that's Han's mother?"

He assured him once again it was and laughed when he left him. Two minutes later, all five of his brothers were in the room with him, as well as his mom. She'd stopped by to see if they'd take her to dinner with Hannah that night and had happened upon this meeting.

"You should get a kick out of this," Andrew told her. "Just don't be surprised if I throw up on you."

"What on Earth...?" When the door opened a minute later, his mom looked at him with the most stunned look on her face. "Misha? What is this?"

"Everyone, I'd like you to meet Hannah's mom." His mom stood up and sat back down. "Mrs. Oliver, what can I do for you?"

"Oh my. All of you at once. Whatever am I to do?" She looked at his mom, who was still staring with her mouth open. "You their pimp?"

"Their mother. And what, may I ask, are you?" Before Bella could answer her, their mom stood up. "You should be ashamed of yourself. What were you thinking when you left your house this morning? Or did you even...good gracious, woman, your breasts are showing, and your...your personal self is nearly hanging out so that anyone could see it."

"I'm just being myself. I like being sexy." Bella sneered at her. "You should try it sometimes. You're not too old yet. Let it hang out."

"Of all the...you're that young woman's mother?" Bella nodded and smiled again. Then she struck a pose that Misha could only assume was supposed to be sexy. "Straighten up and cover yourself. You're too old to be looking like you've just spent a night screwing everything that had a dick."

Andrew laughed, but one look at him from their mother had him shutting up. Bella stood up straighter and nearly fell off her heels when she started forward. But his mom was ready for her.

"Do it and I will rip your eyes out of that overdone face of yours." Bella stopped, and his mom looked at him. "Get her out of here. And don't touch her. I shudder to think what she's been up to for the last twenty-four hours."

Misha and Rider escorted Bella out. She was cursing the entire time, and he and Rider were laughing so hard it was difficult for them to be serious. When Bella stopped moving and looked at them, Misha could see the insanity. It was frightening as much as it was funny.

"You tell that bitch of a daughter of mine I'm not done with her yet. When I find her, she's going to go back to that place and I'm going to have her get one of those brainectomies."

She was out the door when it occurred to him what she'd meant. Misha was still laughing when he entered his office. But seeing his mom handing out bottles of antibacterial hand wash to everyone had him hurting, he was laughing so hard. It was the best thing he'd had happen in months.

CHAPTER 10

Han walked around the yard twice before she ventured into the wooded area behind the house. Mr. Jackson, who she was told to call simply Jackson, said that the property was fenced in and that she should feel free to roam as she wanted. The booted cast she had on was nice since she could walk instead of riding on her butt all the time. And the sun felt wonderful on her face. She looked down at her list.

Han had always wanted an herb garden. She wasn't a great cook by any means, but the smell of some of the richer herbs she'd seen in shops was so nice that she was excited to see if she could find some in the yard. Jackson had given her a small knife, a book on herbs, as well as a basket to put them in. He'd even gone out to the yard and showed her how to dig them up without hurting them.

"You go on and get us some starts. There are wild herbs out there that are just waiting for someone to cut them up in some salad. If you bring back the wrong thing, we'll just toss it and try again." She nodded and left him standing there.

It was the trust, she supposed, that had her liking the older man. He'd told her he was a leopard as well, but she'd shied away from talking to him about her relationship with Misha. Her body warmed at the thought of the things he'd done to her last night. And when she'd been to the doctor this afternoon, Doctor Hudson had commented on how she could take the cast off her arm now because of him biting her. Han put her hand over the small scar she'd found after her shower.

A sound startled her, and she stilled in the woods for several minutes, trying to figure out where it was coming from. Moving slowly, one step at a time, she made her way to just where the broken fence was to see something struggling. Putting her knife in the basket, she dropped it over the fence, and then climbed over it to see what it was.

Han had no idea what to expect, but was still surprised to see a small puppy with its leg caught in a bear-like trap. He was pulling at it so hard that he'd only managed to make it worse rather than to get away. She moved close to him and he snarled at her.

"I'm not going to hurt you. I want to help you." He growled low, and she inched forward. "I'm hurt, too, so helping you will make me feel better. Don't move so much; you're going to make it worse."

The little thing sat down and stared at her, and it was then that she realized it wasn't a dog but a wolf. A black one. As she made her way closer to him, he whimpered when she put out her hand for him. It upset her that he was afraid of her, but he sniffed her, then licked her fingers. Moving closer, she rubbed her fingers over his small head and spoke softly to him.

"I'm not really sure how this works. The trap I mean. And for the record, whoever put this out here needs to have his leg snapped in one." The pup licked her face when she leaned down to look at it. "Has this thing been dipped in silver?"

The thing looked new, but when she got close enough to see how it worked, she could see that it wasn't new at all. The poor thing licked her again when she tried to pull it apart. Finally, after hurting him once so badly that he bit her, she figured it out.

"I'm not going to be able to pull you out of the teeth on this thing and hold it open for you. Do you think you can get your leg out when I get it opened?" She could have sworn that he nodded at her, and she smiled. "I'm really sorry, but I don't think this is going to hurt any less than it does now, but you're not going to be trapped in this any longer."

Taking several deep breaths, she pressed down on the lever until the jaws started to open. It was slow moving for the first few seconds, but then she heard it snap and cried out when the little pup was falling out of it. Letting the trap go, it snapped shut again with such a loud crack that she jumped. But the little pup was trying to get away from it, and she reached for him.

"I can't let you run off like this. What if you get trapped again?" The little guy whimpered again, and she picked him up. "I don't know where your den is, but I'm going to take you back to Misha's house. We'll get you bandaged up and then we'll see what we can do. Misha is a leopard, but...do wolves like cats?"

She rambled on the entire way back toward the house. He never tried to bite her again, for which she was grateful, but it was close a couple of times. She'd nearly dropped him when they crossed over the fence to Misha's property. Then, suddenly, she was being thrown back and had to wrap her body around the pup so he'd not be hurt when she fell.

"That's mine." The big man was standing over her, and he had a gun. "Put my prey down or so help me, you'll take his place. Drop him."

"I most certainly will not." She was terrified, but she wasn't going to let the poor thing go with the man. "You're on someone else's property, and so is he. You get out of here before I call the owner."

"You mean that big man that just bought this place? I'm not worried about him. You should be more concerned with the fact that you took something that belongs to me. Give him over now and I'll only mess you up a bit." The pup snarled at the man, and Han knew just how he felt. When something tingled in her mind, she was startled when Misha spoke to her.

I can feel your fear. What's happening? Is your mother there at the house? I'm on my way. She didn't know what to do to tell him, and he told her to think of what to say. *Just talk to me in your head.*

There's a little wolf here that's been hurt in a big trap. Now there's a man standing over me with a gun demanding that I give him to him. I'm not going to. And if you make me, I'll never...I'll never sleep with you again.

I would never...we seriously need to have a long talk. I'm contacting Jackson. He's on his way. And so am I. When you see the leopard, don't attack him. It will be one of us. She nodded and then told him thanks. *Just don't move. If he hurts you, I'm going to tear him apart.*

There was movement just behind the big man, and Han thought it was Jackson. But the pup in her arms started to struggle again, and she let him go when he nipped at her arm. He grabbed her shirt and started pulling her back when a flash of something dark and large leapt at the man.

Han watched it all. She knew that on some level what she was seeing wasn't something that anyone would believe. She was having trouble believing it herself. But the pack of wolves that tore into the man—and they did tear into him—never looked her way until he was down. She'd seen one man killed like this by another wolf, but nothing like this pack was doing to this man.

Then she knew he was dead. The wolves all circled around him and threw back their collective heads and howled. Instead of being afraid of them, she thought only of their beauty.

The biggest wolf started toward her. The pup moved to stand in front of her, and she pulled him back into her arms. He tried to get away from her, but there was no way she was going to let them hurt the little guy.

"You get back. You try to hurt him and I will find a gun and shoot you all. Get back." The big wolf got close enough for her to touch him, and she smacked him on the nose. "I said to get the hell back. I'm not going to tell you again."

The wolf sneezed but didn't back off. The rest of them stood just behind him, and Han realized she was in deep shit. These guys looked bigger than any wolf she'd ever seen before. She just knew that she was going to be dessert following the big man they'd killed.

"Miss Hannah?" She looked at Jackson, who had come tearing into the woods where they were. When she yelled at him to stop, she looked at the big wolf.

"You don't hurt him either. He had nothing to do with whatever is going on here. You have to hurt someone, you…you can hurt me. But leave him alone." The wolf looked at Jackson, then back at her as he lay down on his belly. The pup finally broke free from her and went to the big wolf. He was tumbling all over him, and she realized that they knew each other. "He's hurt and needs to be helped. Just let me wrap him up before you take him away. He might get infected."

"Miss Hannah, that there is Mr. James Luna. He's the pack alpha that runs through here sometimes." She glanced at Jackson, then back at the wolf. "That pup there is his son. They're shifters like me and the Lannings are."

"The little one is hurt." Jackson moved toward her and the big wolf stood up and moved to stand over her. He growled low in his throat at Jackson, making him stop. "What's he doing?"

"Protecting you from me." She looked at the big wolf, who was so close she could see the green of his eyes. Putting her hand on his neck, she felt his muscles quiver under her fingers.

"He's my friend, Mr. Luna." He turned and looked at her, and she could see the man that held the wolf. When he sat down on her booted foot, she looked at Jackson. "I guess he's not moving."

"Misha is on his way. They know it. They're not going to leave you until then. They can smell him on you." Han flushed, knowing what that meant, but said nothing as Jackson sat down. "I can hear him now. I don't think he's going to be terribly happy when he gets here either. Those brothers of his are with him, too."

Boy was that an understatement. As soon as he crashed through the woods at her, she knew the real meaning of huge and pissed off. Misha moved toward her and she knew, just knew, that he was going to tear her throat out. But the moment he was close enough to touch her, the big wolf moved back, but not far, and Misha rubbed his body all over hers. She'd never seen a more beautiful sight than him as a leopard.

~~~

Misha couldn't stop touching her. He knew that he was irritating her, but she'd been nearly hurt and taken from him, and he was more afraid than he'd been about anything in his life. And now that it was over and she was at the house, all he wanted to do was mark her again. But company demanded that he wait.

"You should know that he bit her." Misha nodded at James. He'd seen the mark, too. "I'm sorry about that. Jimmy, however, thinks it's the best thing in the world that he has a connection with the big leopard mate."

"She might have hurt him." James nodded and looked at Han, who was talking to the other children in the pack. They'd come over as soon as they'd shifted to thank the small human.

"I never seen a woman, much less a human, so furiously want to protect someone she didn't know. I swear to you, Misha, I thought for sure she was going to get up and tear my throat out when I tried to see if my son was all right. I wish I had a dozen more just like her to have bred some of that into my pack."

Misha growled low, and James laughed. "Stay away from my woman. And for the record, I've never…that was the scariest thing I've ever felt in my life, when I felt her fear. And to be honest, it was more for the pup than herself."

James nodded and took the beer that Jackson offered him. But he moved by Misha when he reached for one. Wondering what was going on, he looked at Phillip when he sat down next to him with a bottle of water and handed it to him.

"Did you know that Han hates beer? Can't stand the smell, much less the taste." He nodded to the water. "Drink up, big brother. I just saved your ass."

He wondered how Phillip knew, but realized there was a great deal about his mate that he didn't know. Misha looked over at James. His mate was large with their next child, and he looked at her with such love that Misha wanted to be embarrassed.

"It'll come to you." He asked James what he meant, and he turned to him. "Love. I can see that you're in love with her, but all I see from her is...misunderstanding. She's not sure of the two of you, is she?"

"No." Misha watched her play with the children and smiled when one of them made her laugh. "I haven't been that great of a mate to her as yet. I'm not even sure what I need to do to make her happy. And I find that I really do want to."

"As I said, it'll come to you." He stood up and looked at him. "I need to give your mate a gift. She gave me the greatest gift anyone could ever give to a human or shifter."

"I'm sure she won't see it that way." James looked at her, then back at him. "I give you permission, if that's what you're waiting for, but you don't need it from me. If she accepts whatever you give her, then I will as well."

"That, my dear sir, is a good start." He moved to his mate and helped her to stand. Misha stood up as well and watched as they approached her. Little Jimmy stood just in front of his dad. Misha looked at his brothers and mother as they, too, watched the couple.

"Hannah Oliver Lanning." Hannah looked at Misha, and he nodded at her. "I am the leader of the Luna pack, a pack of just over six hundred wolves. You have, in one selfless action, humbled and honored me in a way that no one has before."

"I didn't do anything but help the little guy out." She looked at Misha, panicky, and he moved to stand behind her. "Anyone would have done the same thing."

"Maybe, but you did it for me. Even at the cost of a bloodied nose." He put his hand on his nose and laughed. "You ever want to wrestle with me, just don't hit me in the nose. It's my best feature I think."

James's mate slapped him gently on the arm and hugged Hannah to her. "You gave us our son. He would have died had you not been brave enough to save him. Then to have taken on that human when he was bent on...." She turned her face into James's chest and sobbed before she continued. "He would be a trophy on his wall had you not fought so bravely to keep him safe for us."

Jimmy looked at Misha, who nodded once and watched as the little boy launched himself at Hannah. He held her so tightly that there wasn't a person in the room that couldn't see how happy he was. Jimmy got down and stood nearby as his father lifted her arm up and looked at the mark that was still there.

"I wish to add my mark to that of my son. So that whenever you are in need of me or my pack, you need only to think of me and we'll drop everything and come to you." Misha put his hands on Hannah's shoulders when she started to back away. "I will never harm you, and so long as I live, no harm will ever come to you."

"You want to bite me?" She sounded so calm when she asked that Misha was proud of her. He alone could feel the turmoil that was dancing in her stiff frame. "And we, you and I, will be able to talk like Mr. Lanning...Misha and I can?"

"Yes. Not on the same level as the two of you but close. You will be able to speak to my mate, Ruby, as well." James laid his hand on her swollen belly. "And our child not yet born, too."

"I don't want to make a big deal of this." James nodded and held onto her hand. "I also don't…will it hurt?"

"No." James pulled her hand to his mouth and licked her wrist. "You'll not feel a thing. I promise."

It was quick. His teeth sank deep into her skin, and he was pulling away almost as soon as he'd done it. Within seconds, less it seemed, Han had a scar on her arm that looked like the one on her shoulder that Misha had given her. And the one on his neck she'd given him. A few minutes later, the wolf pack left and his family sat around, staring at her.

"I'm not a freak." Carter laughed, and then the rest of them joined in when she snapped at them. His mom stood up and hugged her just before she announced that it was time they all left. Each of his brothers hugged her to them, and Rider kissed her cheek then stepped back when it was his turn.

"Welcome to the family, Han. I'm very happy that you're going to tame my brother." Han looked at Misha, and he could see her confusion. He'd really have to have a talk with his family about her. They were not helping him.

After they left, Jackson told them that he would have dinner ready in two hours. He suggested that Han take him out into the yard and show him where the fence was broken down. They were nearing the woods when she turned to him.

"You were there. So why is he getting rid of us?" Misha laughed and led her deeper into the woods. "I don't understand anything that just happened. That little boy was hurt; you would have done the same thing."

"I would have. But I knew he was a little boy and you did not." She didn't say anything as she moved over the fallen logs. He wanted to pick her up and carry her, but watched her move ahead of him instead.

"James said that he was confused by me being only partly human. I don't know what he meant by that." Misha started to explain, but she continued before he could. "You bit me the other night, and I bit you. The doctor said I would heal faster. Now this thing with the wolf. Are you changing me into what you are?"

"I honestly don't know." She stopped moving and turned to look at him. He was caught staring at her ass and flushed when she glared at him. "You cannot blame me for looking. I think you have the nicest bottom I've never seen."

"You shouldn't be thinking of that sort of thing. It's daylight." He looked up at the sky then back down at her when she started moving again. He put his hand on her shoulder to turn her around. There was no way she believed that sex should be only done at night. More than likely in the bedroom as well.

"I want you right now." She shook her head and backed up a step. He caught her up when she started to trip. "I would like nothing more than to strip you down and eat your pussy while you hung onto that tree. Then I'd like to bend you over it, and take you hard from behind."

"No. You can't want to do that. It's not...I don't want it." She had lied and they both knew it. As he flared his nostrils to get more of her scent, he moved her closer to the tree. "You're really going to do this? Now?"

"Yes. Yes I am." He heard her heart rate pick up, her breathing turning into a hard pant. "You want me to as well. You'd come in my mouth if I dropped to my knees and suckled your clit into my mouth while you rode my fingers. I'd drink you down, swallowing you as fast as you flooded my mouth."

"I don't think this is a good place to do this." He lifted her shirt over her head and never took his eyes from her face. She watched him, too, as her fingers curled around his cloth-covered cock and pressed against him. "You make me want things that I've never wanted before. I don't understand this."

"Me neither." Her bra came off next, and he lifted her breasts in his hands as he toyed with her nipples with his thumbs. "Can I eat you, Hannah? Can I feast on your pussy then fuck you?"

"I want that, but…. Yes." He dropped to his knees, pulling her pants down as he moved his mouth over her naked belly. "Please. I want…can you hurry, please?"

Her panties were soaking wet. Misha licked a path from her right hip to the left one before he had her naked. Looking up at her, she'd stretched her hands up and held onto the branch above her head. Lifting her leg up, he rested it on his shoulder as he buried his face in her heat.

She was dripping with juices. They ran down her creamy thighs, and he lapped up as much as he could before he suckled her clit into his mouth. When she cried out, her release gave him so much more of her that he knew that his cock would slide into her without any difficulty. Misha spread her wider for him and fucked her with his tongue.

Hannah came four times before she started to beg him to let her down. Misha stood up and pulled his cock free.

When she reached for him, wrapped her hot hands around him, he moaned. She was going to make him come if she kept it up and he told her so.

"I've never tasted a man before." His cat snarled along his skin, and she jerked back. "He doesn't like me, does he?"

"On the contrary, he loves you as much as I do. And he wants you, too." She stepped back and his cat snarled at him. "He wants to mark you. Taste you as well, but he needs to mark you. He can smell the wolf on you."

"Taste me how?"

He shifted. Misha knew that he'd scared her a little, but she didn't run, for which he was both happy and sad. When his cat moved to her thigh, he thought he was simply going to bite her and be done with it, but he buried his muzzle into her pussy and nipped.

Hannah screamed, not from pain but from the climax that tore from her. When she came a second time, the cat bit deep into her thigh and she screamed again. As she fell to the ground, he never let her go even as Misha begged him to. At some point, he realized that Hannah had fainted, and still his cat held her in his powerful jaws.

Misha couldn't get him to back off, couldn't control the cat, and no matter how hard he tried, he wouldn't stop biting her. Then, as suddenly as he'd bitten her, he let her and him go. Misha shifted and picked her up. Christ, she was as cold as ice. Carrying her to the house, his only thought was that he'd killed her. Then when he got her to the bed, it was all he could do not to panic. Calling his mom was the only thing he could think to do, and she laughed at him.

He's changed her. She'll be fine in about ten hours. In the meantime, if I were you, I'd think of something really nice to give her. Hannah is not going to be happy with either one of you.

Christ, she really was going to be pissed.

CHAPTER 11

Bella was tired of living in the house she'd found. There were no mirrors to start with, and her clothing was getting dirty from all the nasty stuff that was floating in the air. She glared at the bed she had made herself and wondered if that was why she was itching all the time. She was positive that it had fleas and had given them to her. And she was hungry.

The last time she'd had a proper meal was three days ago. And that hadn't been all that good. But the man she'd blown in the alley hadn't said he'd buy her a steak dinner, only that he'd feed her. She'd eaten the cold burger and fries as he drove away. The motherfucker hadn't even given her a napkin.

Bella had to find herself someone to fuck. Not that she wanted sex, far from it, but men paid lots of money to fuck someone like her. She knew this and was trying to figure out a way to capitalize on it when she noticed her picture on one of the newspapers she'd stolen. Pulling it out, she tried to read what it said and could only get about five words into the article when she realized that she needed help.

Taking the paper with her, she went to the lower level where she knew two homeless men lived. She'd tried her best to avoid them, but today she needed their help. As soon as she stepped into what they had told her was their property, the bigger of the two of them stood up.

"You got no reason to come down here spouting off your rules. We ain't touched nothing of yours." The younger man snickered and she glared at him as the big man continued. "You go on out of here. You got your own place."

"I need help reading this." She showed them the paper with her picture on it. "I left my glasses somewhere and I can't see what this here says about me. Can either of you see it?"

"We can read. But before we do that for you, whatcha going to give us in return?" The younger man rubbed his cock. "You give me head and I'll read it to you."

"What about me? I got needs, too." The big man simply pulled down his pants and rubbed his cock up and down. "You come here and give me something and I'll read you the whole thing front to back."

"Do you both?" The younger man nodded, and Bella rolled her eyes. "I'll do you both at the same time to save me some time. I don't care who I blow, but the other one is going to have to settle for a fuck. That way you can read it to me quicker."

"You'll let me fuck your ass?" The big man moved toward her. "I'd love me some ass. Donnie here, his ass ain't fit for my cock no more. I'd like to have me something with a pussy."

She eyed the big man and realized his cock was small in comparison. If he fucked her in the ass, she'd not have to worry about any diseases. Everyone knew that the only way to catch anything was in your pussy. She told him yes.

Donnie sat down on the wire holder that seemed to be in great abundance in this building. She had one that she used as a table. He was apparently going to use his as a bed. He'd already taken his pants off and was fondling himself as he watched her undress. When he held his cock for her, she leaned over and took him as deep as she could and he cried out. The sooner this was over the better.

The man at her ass played with her for a bit. She didn't really care. Maybe if he got enough fingering her pussy, he'd give up on her ass. But she realized too late that he was lubing her up, and he slammed his cock into her ass before she was ready. She screamed out, wondering what the hell he'd stuck in her because he was tearing her apart.

He held her hips in his meaty paws as he fucked her. Every time he pulled back and slammed forward, she felt as if he were at her throat. Something slid down her leg, and she knew it was blood. The man was bigger than anything she'd had shoved in her before, and he was hurting her. When he leaned over her, biting at her shoulder, she felt as if she were going to die. Then Donnie told her he was coming and lifted her head up from him. His cock was in her pussy before she could say a word. The two of them were buried so deep inside of her that she knew that she'd be lucky if she could walk after this.

"You're going to stand real still while we finish." She didn't say anything, and Donnie slapped her. "Answer me, bitch. You gonna give us any trouble now that we're fucking your holes?"

"No." He slapped her again, and she cried. "Please, not my face. It's all I gots." He laughed, and she felt Donnie move out as big man moved forward. They were moving in and out of her so quickly now that she had to hold on to one of them as they enjoyed themselves.

"Oh baby, you got more than your face. You have a tight hole for us and you're going to let us have it." She didn't understand but couldn't ask him as he'd put his hand over her mouth. When he bit into her breast hard enough to draw blood, she screamed again and felt her knees weaken. "Oh no you don't. We ain't nearly done with you yet."

They fucked her back and forth for what seemed like hours. As soon as one pulled nearly out, the other would slam forward. Bella had been bitten by them so many times that she hurt everywhere. When the big man, Bill, Donnie called him, squeezed her nipple hard enough that she was sure he'd pinched it off, she sobbed again when Donnie suckled from it while Bill held it to his mouth. Then Bill started pounding harder, not waiting for Donnie to pull back.

"I'm coming. Christ, I'm coming." Bill pounded while Donnie encouraged him. When he finished, Donnie lifted her legs up while Bill held her shoulders up off the floor, and he fucked her while she was held between them. As soon as he came, Donnie yelled out his own release. She then felt a cock rammed into her mouth, and Bill came down her throat while Donnie laughed.

She was laid out on the wire holder, and they both stood over her. Neither of them looked like they were finished, as they were both still as hard as stone. It was then that she got a good look at Bill's cock. Christ, it was as thick as her wrist and nearly as long as her arm from wrist to elbow.

"I got me a nice one, huh?" He rubbed it over her bloodied nipple, then leaned down and sucked hard on it. "I'm going to enjoy this more than you can imagine. A nice ass you have, but I need to have me some of that pussy."

Donnie laughed as he moved her around on the table. "Yeah, I'm going to have me some pussy, too, but I'm going to eat it. I'm not much of an ass man myself. Unless it's Bill's here. His cock can fill me like none other."

"You're going to rape me?" The men looked at each other, then burst out laughing. "You can't be taking what I'm not offering you. That's against the law. I'll call the cops."

"No, you won't, Belladonna Oliver." She looked at them, wondering how they knew her name. "We done seen the paper with your picture in it. Read all about how you killed some bastard when you bashed his head in with a tire iron. When you kill a man, you shouldn't leave behind your spit. Gave you away right away. All over his dick, my friend said it was. You sucked him good, then killed him. So we figured we'd go on up and get us some of what you're offering. And then there you were, coming to us. We're going to make you our sex slave for a bit."

"No." Donnie slammed his cock into her pussy and smiled at her even as she tried to get away. But Bill held her down while he played with her pussy and Donnie's cock as he slid in and out of her. Bella started to scream, but Bill simply put his cock in her mouth when he got up on the table and mounted her.

"That's it, baby. Suck me off." He rode her like a dog would, and she felt her pussy being licked by him. As soon as he sucked her clit into his mouth, something incredible happened: Bella came. The two men were raping her, and she was fucking enjoying it.

"Come again." The command took her off guard, but she did it. Her body screamed out a release that nearly took her head off. As Donnie yelled he was coming, Bill filled her mouth and throat with his cum and she came again. Bella had never enjoyed sex this much in her life.

"You're going to love this next part." She shook her head, thinking she was satisfied enough for one night, but Bill lay down on the floor and told her to get on him. She didn't hesitate as she staggered over to him and lowered herself over his thickening cock and rode him.

Donnie stood in front of her with his cock in his hand, and she didn't even think but opened her mouth for him. His cock fucked her mouth so deeply that several times she thought for sure she was going to strangle. But then Bill sat up and bit her again, and her pussy tightened around him in another climax. Bella came twice more before either man came again.

They'd had sex in every position they could think of by the time they declared they were finished for tonight. And some positions she was sure they were making up. Her entire body hurt, and she'd never been so relaxed in her life. As she lay between the two of them on the two mattresses they had, she felt a cock nudge her in the ass and knew it was Donnie. When he slowly moved in and out of her, Bill turned and played with her pussy.

"Tomorrow we're going to have us some more fun." She nodded as she felt her climax build up. "Then we might have a few friends over to have some fun, too. You'll love Jack; his cock is bigger than mine but not as long. And the things he could do with it will have you begging like a bitch in heat."

Bella could hardly wait. She saw the newspaper lying where she'd dropped it and started to ask one of them to read it, but she really didn't care right now. When Donnie came a few minutes later, she wrapped her arms around Bill and closed her eyes. She might have to buy herself a house and keep these guys around for a while. Smiling, she fell asleep.

~~~

Hannah woke up and lay there for several seconds while she tried to think why she felt so strange. Doing a quick inventory of everything, she felt better than good, she felt great. Opening one eye to see if she was alone, she looked at the man staring at her. She sat up just enough to make him out.

"Rider Lanning?" He saluted her but said nothing. She started to sit up and realized she was naked. "Where's Misha?"

"In the shower. He was smelling pretty bad, so we told him we weren't going to bring him up any more food until he cleaned up. He's been in here with you for three days." She looked around the room and didn't recognize it. "This is Misha's room. You've been recuperating for a few days."

"Recuperating? Recuperating from what?" Rider just smiled. She was beginning to dislike this man. "Are you going to tell me or do I need to find Misha?"

"I'm not telling you. Not because you don't need to know. It's just that we're taking bets on whether or not you murder him, castrate him, or simply leave him. All of which have good odds. My mother thinks you're a sensible girl and will be fine." She wondered what he was talking about, but knew asking wasn't going to get her anywhere. He was enjoying this too much.

He'd bitten her. Misha's cat had…he'd hurt her, and he'd bitten her hard. Things came to her slowly and then she remembered something that Carter had told her. She knew then what had happened. She was a leopard.

"I'm going to get up and find him. I'm assuming that he's in the bathroom here." Rider nodded. "And you might know or not that I'm naked. When I get up, you're either going to be gone or get an eyeful."

Rider stood up. "Have you figured it out?"

"Yes. Is everything…did it work?" He shrugged. "Any suggestions on how to turn into a cat? I'd like to see if it worked before I freak out."

"Summon her. She's right there. You just have to think of her and call her to you." He leaned down and kissed her forehead. "I lost a hundred bucks. I thought you'd want to murder him."

"I still might. But I can do more damage as a cat than as me, right?" He laughed as he left the room, and she said his name. Turning back, she looked at him. "Is your family pissed off?"

"On the contrary, they're very happy for you both." She nodded, and he smiled. "It's really too bad you aren't going to at least hurt him. But you should know, Hannah, that he does love you."

He moved out of the room, shutting the door behind him. Han felt her energy levels soar at the thought of changing and closed her eyes. The cat, huge and beautiful, sat there staring at her, as if she knew that it was time.

"You ready for this?" The cat stretched out and then yawned. Han laughed. "Come to me. Take me."

It was almost like she moved over her. She felt her arms stretch out, her fingers ached a little, and then she was down on the floor. She looked at the bathroom door and realized that she should have checked that first, but found the door opened enough she could get her paw in. He was indeed in the shower.

She had no idea what to do. Looking at the counter, she leapt up onto it and sat down. It really wasn't big enough for her, but she was determined to make sure he saw her when he came out. Turning her head slightly, she saw herself.

Her fur wasn't like Misha's. It was white, but the spots that he had were all over him. She looked like someone had splashed a little paint on her and missed for the most part. Her eyes were darker than her normal blue, but nothing like Misha's were. He had the most gorgeous eyes she'd ever seen. The water turned off, and she turned to see him push the door back.

"Christ." He stared at her for several seconds before he spoke again. "How do you feel? I'm really sorry that—"

Han growled, feeling the vibration come all the way from her tail. When he reached for the towel on the hanger, she growled again. He stepped back when she swiped her paw at him when he reached again.

"I have to dry off." She didn't move until he tried a third time. "Look, I know that you're pissed, but I'm at a great disadvantage here in that I'm fucking naked and you're not. Unless you want me to shift and go with you."

Sounded like a plan. Leaping off the counter, she moved toward him, and Misha backed away. She liked this newfound power she had and nipped at his thigh. When he grabbed his cock, she licked his hands.

"You're playing with fire, Hannah. I'd like nothing better than to shift with you and run in the woods. But if you're planning to bite my dick, we're both going to be hurting." She looked up at him, and she watched his face. "Do you have any idea how absolutely beautiful you are right now?"

She moved out of the room and to the bedroom door. Han was still sitting there when he came out with the towel around his waist. As he moved toward her she stood up, and when he was close enough, she purred, rubbing her body over his legs. As soon as the door opened, she was out the door and down the stairs. Han heard him laughing as she slipped twice on the hallway rugs.

Han didn't think to expect others to be in the kitchen. And they were all there, too. Maribel was sitting at the table drinking tea, but the men, all six of them, including Jackson, were standing around her. Han stopped when one of them moved toward her.

"I'm only going to open the door." There were footsteps coming behind her, and she dashed to the door. She heard them laughing as she leapt off the deck and onto the ground below.

Han felt amazing. Her entire body felt like it had been given a boost of something powerful. She ran as fast as she could and only stopped when she saw the fence line just in front of her. Turning hard to the right, she jumped over logs and big rocks. Each time, she came down on her paws, only to kick them up again in what seemed like flight. Han wanted to take on the world. When she finally stopped and lay down, she felt someone come up behind her and turned to look at Misha. His cat was walking slowly, as if he had not a care in the world.

You enjoying yourself? She nodded as best she could. *We can speak this way, just like before; think of me and I'll hear you.*

I've never felt this wonderful in my life. I can jump over everything. Well, not everything, but I didn't fall. And my body feels like I can take on anyone. I won't, but Christ, I feel...I feel fantastic. He laughed, and she felt embarrassed. *I'm sorry. You must think I'm an idiot. It's just that I've never done anything like this before. To you it must be old news.*

No. It's wonderful to see this through your eyes. I'm glad you're okay with this. She stood up when he was closer to her, and her cat wanted him. Moving along his body, she purred deep in her throat while she walked around him twice more. *You're going to make me want you more than I already do.*

You mean have sex this way? He nipped at her shoulder when she walked by him. *How would that even work? I mean, I guess it happens. Do you mount me?*

Yes. He stopped her this time by biting into her shoulder. Her cat, taking exception to it, she supposed, snarled at him, but he didn't let her go. *I need you.*

Please. He let her go long enough to order her to lie still. Turning so that her ass was under him, he moved up behind her, and she lifted her ass up. He pressed her into the dirt with his big paw, and she felt him nudging her from behind. As soon as he entered her, his cock filling her, she felt him bite her again, this time deep in her other shoulder.

Do you have any idea how you feel to me right now? He took her hard, his cock pistoling in and out of her more quickly than he'd ever done before. *I'm going to fill you like this, fill your body with my cum. Then we're going to shift, and I'm going to take you like you've never had me take you before.*

Her pussy was aching, she wanted him so badly. And when he came, she cried out in frustration as he growled at her to be still. Han snarled at him when he backed from her.

"Shift, Hannah. I need you." He was standing over her, naked now. His cock, thick and hard, was stretched out before him, and she felt her mouth water. When he told her again to shift, she closed her eyes and felt herself become human. Misha nearly fell atop her when she rolled to her back.

"I'm going to eat you." She nodded as he lifted her legs up to his shoulders. "When you come, I'm going to drink you until I've had my fill. Then I'm going to fuck you. It'll be hard. You're going to love it."

"Because I'm a cat." He didn't answer her but lifted her pussy to his mouth. He watched her as he slid his tongue into her and fucked her.

He ate at her lips, her clit. Her thighs were bitten, and she came twice before she could catch her breath. Lowering her to the ground, he continued to eat her until she felt as if she would never be able to walk. Then he lifted his head and sat back on his heels. She watched him as he fisted his cock.

"I want to lick you. Could I taste you like you have me?" He nodded, and she moved to sit in front of him. When he stood up, she ran her fingers up his thighs to his cock and cupped him in her hands. "So hard and silky. I never thought of a man being so thick like you are. I never thought you'd fit."

"You're tight, but you can handle me." She licked just the tip to catch the pearl of cum that was there. "You're going to have to either let me fuck you, love, or take me into your mouth. I can't—"

She wrapped her mouth around him, and he cried out. The taste of him, the heated sex, made her want more. When he curled his hand into her hair and showed her how to take him, she moaned at the flavor of his cum as more of it slid down the back of her throat.

"Swallow me." She didn't understand at first, but when he pushed to the back of her throat and gagged her, she swallowed then and he cried out. "That's it. Christ, I'm going to come. Baby, if you don't want to drink my cum, stand back and I'll release on you."

She held him by his hips and he came, his cock sliding in and out of the back of her throat. She cupped his balls in her hand and held them as they emptied. When Misha was finished, he staggered back from her. She was so needy that she reached for him again.

"I need to be inside of you." She nodded, not really caring how he took her so long as he did. "I want to mount you again, but I need to...do you have any idea how gorgeous you are? I can't decide how to fuck you, only that I need to."

Han lay on her back and spread her legs open. As he stood over her, she ran her fingers down over her breasts to her belly. He never stopped watching her fingers as she danced them over each nipple before sliding back to her navel.

"Now spread your pussy for me. Play with your pretty clit while I watch you." His voice, smooth and deep, made her juices flow. Not even caring that she'd never done anything like this before, she spread herself open for him with one hand as she slid her finger over her sensitive nub. She moaned at the feeling and did it again and again.

His breath on her leg was the only warning she got before he suckled her clit into his mouth. When she started to pull her fingers back, he told her no, not to stop. She played with herself while he licked and suckled at her until she was about to burst open.

Misha moved up her body then, taking bites of her skin and licking the small wounds until they were better. He rolled his tongue into her navel several times before he moved up to her breasts and nibbled just on the tips. His cock slid in and out, just to the tip and back, while he played.

"Misha, please?" He looked down at her, his cock stilled. "Please? I ache so much. I need to come."

"Say it again." She started to beg him again, anything to get to have the release that seemed right on the edge, when he said for her to say his name.

"Take me, Misha." His cock took her breath away when he slammed home. And that was what it felt like, too; he was home. Then when he took her mouth, she wrapped her ankles around him and held him to her as he pounded hard, deep within her. His tongue ran along her shoulder to her neck, and she knew he was going to bite her. As soon as he sank his teeth into her, she screamed out his name, crying out her release over and over before biting him. His roar brought her again and again. Han held him while he came a second, then a third time, before she let him go. Her arms fell to the earth, and her legs dropped from his body. Han couldn't move.

He pulled her to him, rolling to his back so that she was on top of him. Closing her eyes, she let herself drift off. Right now, she had not a care in the world, and anyone who wanted her could fuck off. She had never felt better.

CHAPTER 12

The phone ringing nearly made him snarl. But when Hannah giggled behind him and reached over him to answer it, he lay there enjoying her body spread over his. When she handed him the phone, he wanted to tell whoever it was to leave them alone, but he knew that duty called.

He took down the information while she got up from the bed. It was dark in the room, but he could still see that she was wonderfully naked. As she pulled a shirt over her head, he finished up the call and looked at her sitting in the chair.

"I have to go away." She nodded and smiled at him. "You could at least put up a little fight over it."

"If you leave now, you'll be back all the sooner." He stood up and put his hand around his cock. "If you come near me with that, you aren't going anywhere."

He stood there fisting his cock until he heard her heart rate pick up. But he knew as well as she did that he had to go now, not after a quickie. She slid off the chair and, on her knees, came toward him.

"I could help you out if you promise to do the same for me when you get back." Before he could tell her yay or nay, she'd taken him into her mouth and swallowed him down. He didn't want it to be quick; he wanted her to take her time, all damned day if she wanted. But when she cupped his balls and gave them a slight twist, he felt his body react as if she'd commanded him to come. He shouted out her name as he came hard and fast. Sitting back on the bed, he reached for her.

"You should know that I can't leave you hanging." He slid his fingers into her pussy and felt her heat. "You're so wet I could take you now and slide deep."

"I need to come." He nodded and leaned over her. Biting her clit just hard enough to have her cry out, he slid his finger into her pussy, then one into her tight little hole. She screamed this time, her body bowing up off the bed when she came screaming his name. Leaving her now was going to be the hardest thing he'd ever done. Standing up, he smacked her gently on the thigh and told her to behave.

"Do you need to pack?" He leaned his head out of the shower to tell her no, they were always packed and ready to go. "I went down to the kitchen to tell Jackson you were leaving and he's making coffee and rolls for you to take. He said that normally no one wakes him. Should I have let him sleep? He really seems excited to help you out."

"If he bitches too much, next time we'll let him sleep." He took the tea from her as he finished his shower and thought he could really get used to this. By the time he came out of the bathroom, dressed and ready to go, she'd left the room.

When he got to the kitchen, Rider and Phillip were having some warm rolls and coffee. While he was scarfing down his own, the other three showed up, too. Hannah had called them and said to meet there for something to eat. By the time they were ready to roll out the door, she'd packed them a bag of the rolls and two thermoses of drinks: one coffee and one tea. Rider said he'd bring his own thermos next time.

Fifty-three minutes after the call came in, they were in the car to go. Misha stopped the car, then ran to the house. Han asked him if he'd forgotten anything. He told her he had.

Pulling her into his arms, he put as much passion and need into the kiss as he could. Her body went limp against his, and he felt his cock thicken. Oh, to be in bed again with this woman. When he lifted his head, she smacked him softly and smiled.

"Hurry back." He nodded and ran back to the car. Misha had never felt better in his life. That's when he realized that not one of his brothers had teased him about the kiss.

"She's good for you. And damn, she can make a cup of tea!" Rider leaned back on the seat as he continued. "I think that if I ever get a mate, I want one just like her. Quiet and reserved and good in bed."

Misha wasn't sure about the quiet and reserved part. When they'd gotten back into the house last night, she'd torn into him like she was going to murder him about changing her. Christ, he'd been so afraid at one point that he'd nearly called his brothers to protect him. He now had a list of rules he had to follow, or she told him she'd make him regret breaking them for the rest of his lonely, no sex life. He had them memorized.

"She doesn't want children. Not right away anyway. She's afraid." Carter asked him why, and he looked at his brother in the rearview mirror. "She thinks she'll be a mother like hers. She doesn't want to fuck up a child of her own."

"I doubt she would, and she's not her mother." They all looked at Andrew when he spoke. "She stole her, I think. There is no record of anyone ever being born named Hannah Marie Oliver. And as far as I can tell, there is no such person as Belladonna Oliver either. And trust me, I looked hard. There was a child born in the hospital where she told Carter she was from, but it died in childbirth. I think that's our Hannah."

"And her parents? Didn't they look into it?" Rider looked at him as he continued. "You know anything about this?"

"Nope."

In a general sort of there-is-no-fucking-way-that's-her-mother kind of way, Misha had wondered about their relationship, but he had only been thinking that they were so different. He looked at Andrew as they spilled out of the car and hurried to the waiting plane. As soon as they were in the air, he asked him what he knew.

"Nothing much yet. Carter asked me to look into it about the time we figured out she was your mate. I'd already started the process and decided that I'd not find anything and moved on. But the first thing I got back said that she didn't exist. Even her Social isn't right. She's been using a dead woman's since she's been working. And before you ask, I did mention it to Han, but only in that I had paperwork to fill out for the hospital. She gave it to me again and said her mother had applied for it for her when she was in high school." Andrew got his briefcase and took out a few sheets of paper. "I did find this just last night. There was a huge accident just about eight miles from the hospital. Nineteen people were killed when a bus collided with a van. There were so many people coming in from it that somehow her birth got missed. The only thing I can figure is that her mother was on the bus when it crashed, gave birth, and died. No one filed anything, and the baby came up missing because they either didn't know or simply didn't care."

"And Mrs. Oliver took her, you think?" Andrew nodded. "How is this even possible? I mean, didn't anyone know that she was pregnant? Didn't her family wonder what had happened to the child?"

"Best I can piece together, and this is still something that we're working on, is that Han's mother was a runaway and on the bus from somewhere else but died here. Her name was…let me see." Andrew looked over another file of papers as Misha waited. "Deidra Summer. I have someone looking into where she might have come from, but she was riding the bus out of town when it occurred. She's the only one whose body was never claimed. I don't think that was her real name either."

"Where are you looking now?" He told him every place the bus stopped until they found where she got on. "And no one thought to do this before?"

"As I said, it was a huge accident. There were bodies everywhere. According to the police report—and you have to remember this was over twenty-five years ago—several of the men working it had been brought in from the local police academy. Two of the young men dropped out so they'd never have to encounter that again." Andrew handed him a picture. "Then there is this."

The picture was of a young woman that was obviously deceased. Her face looked beautiful, but there was damage done to her torso. Nothing else showed on the picture but the chest to just above her breasts and her face. She looked so much like Hannah that it was breathtaking. Misha wished he knew the color of her eyes, because he knew without a doubt this was Hannah's mom.

"That, in case you don't know, is the woman that no one claimed. I've made inquiries, but no one took a blood sample from her, so I've been trying...I've called in a few favors and I'm having her body exhumed. I sort of told a big fib about why I needed it. I said your wife...she will be soon, right?" Misha nodded without taking his eyes from the picture. "I told them that your wife was wondering about having children and if there was anything in her past. I said we already assumed this woman was her mom. They're going to do it next week."

He kept the picture and asked to be kept informed. Misha felt both excited and afraid for Hannah. To know that the woman wasn't her mother was going to go a long way to making her feel better, but to not know where she came from was something else altogether. She might have a family out there that had mourned her passing all these years. By the time the plane landed, he'd come to a decision. He would tell Hannah, of course, and he'd do it face to face. This was something that had to be done when he could see her, not through their link or on the phone.

~~~

Han waited in the line with Maribel. She'd really wanted to go to this interview on her own, but she didn't know how to drive. As they stood in line—a cattle line, Maribel had called it—Han saw someone out of the corner of her eye that made her stiffen.

"Who is it?" Maribel stood in front of her, and Han felt her cat stir. She didn't know what do to when her fingers started to tingle. Maribel took her chin and had her look at her. "Calm her by talking to her. Tell her it's fine, you have a handle on it. And breathe. That's what has her nervous.

And a nervous cat wants to protect you. Breathe, Hannah. Just breathe."

"It's my mother. She's just over there." Maribel turned her so that her back was to her, and Han took a deep breath. "She's with two men I've never seen before. I don't want to go back to her."

"And you won't, either. I see her now. What a piece of trash. That woman needs to take a serious look at herself when she leaves the house." Han laughed, and Maribel smiled. "There's my girl. Now, tell me what you want to do. If we have to kick her ass, I need to find some more comfortable shoes. These heels are not made for that."

"Are you always this nice?" Han flushed at what she'd said. "I'm sorry. That was very rude of me."

"No, it was you. And I hope to see more and more of you coming out. You're a very wonderful woman, and I'm looking forward to having you do more things with me. Having a woman around will be nice for them as well."

"I don't know about that. I like Carter and Phillip. Andrew is very…he's a sweetheart and so funny. Thomas is quiet and we can sit and play chess for hours without saying a word." She moved up in the line as she thought how to talk about Rider. "I don't think he likes me. Rider, I mean. He's very hard to get to know."

"I noticed that you left out Misha." Han flushed hotter. "He's a good man, too. A little on the jaded side at times. That's my fault. I leaned on him a great deal, as I've said before. But Rider doesn't hate you. I think he's in awe of you." She shook her head. "He is. The other morning he told me that if he had to have a mate, he hoped she'd be like you."

"Why on earth would he want someone like me?" Maribel laughed, and Han joined her. "I'm strange, backward, and I don't know a thing about anything."

"Not true. I understand you speak fluent French, play a hell of a game of chess, and you are good at crossword puzzles, all the things that make me think you're a great deal smarter than anyone has ever given you credit for." Han looked away as she moved to be next in line. "Why on earth are you going to take this job? It's well beneath you, and you could do anything. This is not for you."

"I need to work. I can't sit at Misha's house all day and do nothing." Maribel huffed. "Well, I can't live off him either. He may have money, but I'm not going to sponge off him. I have to work to pay for what I want."

"Okay, I can see that. But you must know that he'd give you whatever you wanted. As for sponging off him? I don't know if you realize just how wealthy they are, all my boys. They've done very well with their money and have a lovely nest egg." Han's number was called, and she looked at Maribel.

"What do I do then? Be a woman that I hate? The kind that comes through the airport as if she owns the world and has nothing to show for it? Do I pop out a kid every few years and hope that Misha never gets tired of me?" Han looked around the room. "There are people in here that need this job more than me, but I need something."

"Work for the Lanning Rescue." Han looked at her then. "Answer the phones during the day. File those reports that sit on their desks for days at a time because no one wants to go to the office downtown. Make coffee and let Misha chase you around the desk."

"And the rest?" Maribel huffed again. "You do that well. Does it work with the others? I just find it to be annoying."

A quick kiss on her cheek and Maribel was leading her from the building. "One, Misha won't tire of you. He loves you very much and will never tire of you. Two. Popping out children? That would be lovely for all of us. But try to have a girl. I'd love a little girl to spoil just once. Three. Yes, it annoys them to no end, but unlike you, they're afraid of me. I'll have to work harder on making you fear me. As for the job, please take it. I hate it. I want to go to flower clubs, join a book of the month group, and have time to knit. I don't know how, but I could learn."

"You're nuts, has anyone ever told you that before? And lived to tell about it?" Maribel shook her head as they got into the limo that pulled up just as they exited the building. "You planned this, didn't you?"

"I did. And now we're going shopping. As flattering as Misha's shirts look on you, I think you need some new things of your own. And before you start bitching about not wanting to spend the money, I am the matriarch of this family and you will do as I say."

They were driving toward who knew where when Han thought of her mother. She'd never taken her shopping that she could remember. And the only time Han ever got new clothes was when she got new uniforms. When she thought of that, she sort of hurt for it. Han looked over at Maribel.

"I don't love Misha. You know that right?" Maribel shrugged, and Han felt frustrated. "He tells me that a lot. That he loves me. I'm not sure he should be doing that when we both know that this relationship is only going to end in heartache."

"My mate was a man much like Misha was just before you came into his life. Not so much cold and heartless, but not caring. Even after the boys started to come into the world, he treated me, and them, too, I suppose, as if we were nothing more than an inconvenience to him. Something that—and I say this with a very heavy heart— something that he must tolerate but never love." Maribel took out her wallet and handed her a picture. It was of the boys when they were younger, all of them handsome and all of them frowning. "Their father wanted that picture. He said that when other people asked him about his kids, he wanted something to prove he had them. There is not a smile among them. Do you know why?"

"He asked them not to be happy and smiling?" Han tried to hand it back, but she shook her head. "I'm sure he loved them at least a little."

"Not at all. He even told them that whenever he could. Then Misha and Rider, well, they stopped saying it to anyone, including me." Han looked up from the picture to Maribel. "Until the other morning. Rider came into the kitchen where I was and kissed me on the cheek. He said in a normal voice, as if he'd said it to me a thousand times that morning, that he loved and cherished me. As he moved out of the room, I stood there so stunned that I could scarcely breathe. Then today, just before Misha left with the others, he came over to my house and hugged me up like a big old bear. Then he told me that he loved me more than he thought possible."

"And you think I had something to do with this?" Maribel nodded. "I don't see how. I barely know Rider, and Misha and I are just...I think it's the sex. He seems to enjoy it a great deal. Perhaps he's just overjoyed because of that."

Maribel laughed, and Han flushed. The things that popped out her mouth lately were strange to say the least. Before she could tell her again how sorry she was, Maribel hugged her.

"You are the best thing that could have happened to all of them. And as much as you want to deny it, I do believe you are just a little in love with them as well. Especially Misha." Han shook her head.

"We aren't in love." Maribel only nodded. "We aren't. We're just two people who have been thrown together because of some twisted fate thing. I don't believe in love."

"Just because no one has loved you before now, my dear, does not mean that you can't have it. You're a wonderful young woman. And one that I will enjoy having around for a very long time." The door to the limo opened, and Han looked at the front windows of the shop before looking back at Maribel. "Are you going to complain and not let me help you pick out clothing? It will do you no good, just so you know."

"You're going to do it anyway, aren't you?" She nodded, and Han felt herself smile a little. "I think I like you, Maribel. You're bossy and a pain in the butt, but you're all right."

"Get it straight, dear. I'm a pain in the ass. Now, we're to spend the day shopping. Which personal item do you need more than anything else? We'll get that first and then buy things to match them." Han asked her why her underthings had to match her outer clothing. "Because, my dear child, you have a mate who will wonder what you have beneath it every time you step into a room." Before she could comment—and what she might have said was still a mystery to her—they were helped out of the limo and escorted into the store. Han felt like she was in a faerie land and she wasn't all that thrilled about it.

They were shown to a small room where there were several mirrors around in sets of three. Before she sat with Maribel, a young man, Toddi, took her to a salon and measured her. He tisked a great deal, and Han wondered what he was finding wrong. Asking him seemed to upset him.

"You are an almost perfect four. I say almost because you have large breasts. If you were perhaps a size or two smaller, then you'd be perfect. Now I'll have to work around this imperfection." She quirked a brow at him. "I'm sure your husband loves them very much, but dressing you will be a nightmare. Come, let's start."

Start was exactly what they did. Like a flagger at a race, when he clapped his hands, several women came forward and started pulling her clothing off. Even her hair was lifted and measured. Han had never been touched by so many people in so many places, and she finally gave up on trying to be modest.

It seemed like hours. She'd been stripped of her clothing, put into a lovely robe, and then taken to have her hair done. Han had no say in that either, and when asked who her stylist had been, she told him.

"When it gets too long, I just hack it off. I have to have it out of my face and sometimes a ponytail is just a bother." She almost laughed at the expression on his face. "You should have seen it when I tried to color it."

She hadn't, of course, but it made her laugh when he staggered back from her. Maribel was moved when she was and sat with her when the man started cutting at her hair. They talked about small things. What her favorite color was, which she had no idea, and did she like heels.

"I have no idea. I've never had any." The man cutting her hair lifted her chin up and looked her in the eye. "I sort of grew up strangely. My mother wore these heels that made me think that I'd never be able to walk in them."

"It's all an art, honey. I'll show you when you get this mop taken care of. And if I hear of you chopping at your hair again?" He fanned himself with the comb. "Well, just don't let me hear about it. You have gorgeous hair, and I'm going to make that mate of yours sit up and pant. Oh my, yes, he will."

Lunch was served when she was under the dryer. The biggest rollers she'd ever seen were currently in her hair, yet she didn't mind so much. No one had let her see herself, and while the two women did her nails and toes, she enjoyed things that she'd never eaten before…shrimp cocktail and brie. There were small sausages as well as the prettiest bread she'd ever eaten. By the time the dryer was off, she was stuffed and ready to move on. It was nearly five o'clock when she was declared ready to have a look.

The mirrors were unwrapped and she was stood in front of them. Han actually looked behind her to see who this woman was. Turning to her right, then left, she fell in love with the green silk dress and the tiny, little-heeled shoes. Maribel put a lovely necklace at her throat, and Han felt tears.

"You mess up my makeup and I'll spank your bottom." Han nodded at Toddi. "I'm to assume you like the butterfly that I've created?"

"Oh yes. It's…I can't believe that's me." He kissed her cheek and stood beside her. "You did an amazing job."

"Oh honey, you've no idea, but we've only just started. You're going to make runway models simply drool when I'm finished with my masterpiece." He grinned. "All I ask for is a description of that mate of yours face when he sees you the first time."

Han wondered if he'd notice, then decided that he'd have to be blind not to. As soon as they left for dinner, she thanked Maribel, who told her not to worry…it was the best fun she'd had in years.

"It was the most fun I've had since I was born."

CHAPTER 13

The death toll was well over two dozen. Not as many as they'd first thought there would be, but enough to exhaust him and his brothers. The town needed a better tornado alert system put in; that might have saved a great many more. But finding the children when they had had done a great deal to boost morale.

"That was just a stroke of luck." Misha didn't look at the mayor, who had been a pain in the ass since they'd arrived over seventy hours ago. "You said they were there, told me over and over they were. I guess that's why you get the big bucks. Knowing your job."

"We do know our job." He grinned at Carter, who had been getting sharper and sharper with the man since they'd found the small room where the nineteen children, all kindergarteners, had been stuffed when the building had been hit. The teacher hadn't faired so well.

"Yeah, so you said, so you said. But it was there, just like you said it would be." Carter moved away, and if his looks were any indication, he did it before he hit the man. "How did you know there was a shelter under all that rubble? The public is going to ask me, and I want to make sure I have all the details. Details make the man, they say."

"Do they?" He nodded, and Misha continued packing up as he answered the man. "It was on the map. The one you told us was outdated. Make sure you let the public know that you would have let them die rather than listen to someone who knew the area. It's a good bet that someone else might know a little more than you."

"I suppose that could be true, but I did call you gentlemen in. So, in effect, when I tell the press that I was instrumental in finding them, it will all be true." Misha paused and turned to look at him. "I'm up for reelection. This will be a feather in my cap, I think. People can be so fickle when things aren't just how they think they should be."

"What do you mean?" He waved Misha off, and he decided to make it his business to find out. After the man left, he called the office to speak to his mom. Instead of her answering, he realized it was Hannah.

"You're there with my mom?" She told him she'd gone to a book club. "So you're filling in for her?"

"I'm working here. Unless you think I shouldn't. I know that people will think it weird that we're working in the same office, but your mom can be very persuasive when she wants to be." He agreed with that one. "I have it down pat, I think. And she only just left me today. I've been doing this for a few days now. Is everything going well there?"

"I called to see if you can find something for me. I have a mayor here that is going to ride into the next election on our coattails. Not that I really care, but I think he's up to something no good and I want to make sure." He gave her his name and where they were. She laughed.

"Up to no good is more like it. He's nearly ready to be impeached. There's a long article in the newspaper about how he's been not only skimming funds allotted for other jobs, but has been taking entire monies earmarked for other projects and buying himself new homes." She laughed again. "His mistress and his wife have been seen fighting in a very public way recently, too. He seems to think that he is entitled to all he's been taking simply because they have been voted nicest city to live in."

"How the hell does he expect to be reelected on that sort of thing?" She told him there was more and sent the links to some articles to his and Rider's phones. His mother had barely been able to get the printer to work, and now he was getting links on his phone. "Are you seriously wanting to work for us?"

"If you don't mind. Your mom took me to the bank and had my signature put on the checks, but I didn't sign anything. The bills are on your desk waiting for you to approve them. Two of them are very past due." He told her to sign them and mail them all. "But I might have done something wrong."

"I highly doubt that. And the fact that I don't have to fuck with it is wonderful. Rider will more than likely buy you whatever you want simply because with you there, he won't have to do it when it's his turn next month." Misha told her how much they all hated the job and traded it around monthly so no one person had to do it all the time. "I trust you, and I know the others do as well. Mail the checks. Anything else?"

He saw Rider coming toward him with a huge smile. He knew that he'd gotten the link. He pointed to his phone and mouthed, "Mom?" Misha shook his head and handed him his phone. When he realized who it was, Rider looked at him, surprised. They talked for a few more minutes until she put him on hold to answer the phone.

"She's working for us?"

Misha said, "Yes" and asked if he was okay with that.

"Are you fucking nuts? I'd have her baby if that were possible. Christ, I have a link and I was so excited that Mom had figured it out that I was ready to buy her a dozen roses. I'm glad now that I waited to ask you if you wanted to go in on them. Han needs something really nice if she's going to work for us."

When she came back on the line, he could hear the tension in her breathing. He felt his cat, always on the surface when they were helping out, run along his skin. He stepped away from Rider when she started talking.

"My mother just called here. How did she know I was here? She said that she's going to come and get me and that I'll be locked up so tightly that they'll never find the key." He started to tell her to calm down but hated that when people said it to him. Instead, he let her talk. By the time she was running down, he could hear her anger instead of her fear.

"What right does she have to tell me that I'm no good? I'm a wonderful person. I have a good job. I don't know how much it pays, but that's beside the point. I have one. And her telling me that she still owns me just doesn't work either. I'm a grown woman. A woman who has a mate. I'm a...I'm a flipping cat. What is she? I'll tell you what she is. She's a mean vicious woman who drinks too much and doesn't know a good thing when she has it."

"Hannah, I love you." She steamrolled right over him and continued, but the words she said before she continued on her tirade had him reaching for something to hold onto.

"I love you, too. But how am I supposed to be able to feel safe when she's done nothing but make my life a living hell? I mean, she nearly killed me this time when she hit me. And then there is that man that was here today."

"What man?" He felt his body tense up, her declaration of love nearly forgotten. "Who was he and what did he want?"

"He said he worked for the police department, but I recognized him from the other day when your mom and I went shopping. He could…you didn't tell me I could smell things and remember them. Anyway, he was in here telling me I had to go with him to the station. I told him to fuck off. Then I called them. The police, not him. They have had a man sitting in the lobby for two days now. If I'm here, he told me, then he's here. His name is Tony Fitzgerald, and a friend of Thomas." Misha went to find Thomas and ask while listening to Hannah. "I've checked him out as well. He is real, and he told me so long as you guys were out of town, he was guarding me. He said he owes Thomas."

And now Misha owed him. As soon as he found Thomas, he was going to find out what it was, but for now, he was just glad that she was being protected. He noticed that she was quiet.

"You do know that I can take care of myself now, right?" Before he could tell her he did know, she continued. "Your mom has been showing me all kinds of things I can do now. And I've been practicing. Even Jackson has been letting me practice in the house. But I'm no longer allowed to be a cat in the living room."

"Why not?" He laughed a little, thinking that whatever she'd done couldn't be that bad. When he heard her sigh, he started to rethink that. "What did you do?"

"The couch…was it anything you really liked? I didn't have any idea that my claws would be out when I stretched. There needs to be a manual on these things. Anyway,

Jackson said that he could repair the one cushion, but when he startled me, I sort of…well, you might need to replace the chair as well. I'll pay you back. I swear."

"I don't care about the cost." He started laughing. "What did you do to the chair? And what were you doing in the house as a cat anyway?"

"Is that another rule?" He told her no, that he was just curious. "I like the way she makes me feel. Like I can take on the world. I know I can't, but I feel safe as her. Jackson said it was fine, he knew how I felt. Did you know that he'd been beaten by his father a long time ago when he was a kid?"

"I did. That's why we're good friends." He was surprised that Jackson had told her about his childhood. Few knew the story. "I'll be home in the morning. We have something here we have to take care of. Then we'll be out. Are you going to be home or at the office?"

He wanted her home, in the bed, naked, but he knew that paperwork had to be filed and there had to be an accounting of what they'd found and done. Especially when they were finished with the mayor.

"Here. I have two appointments lined up for the early morning. I've talked to your mom once or twice since you guys have been gone about some things that need to be worked on, and she said she could approve them. The computer systems here need to be updated. And there is a problem with the furnace. She told me you wouldn't care if I got them taken care of."

He already loved having her there. The furnace had been on its last legs last fall, and the computers had needed an overhaul for years. But none of them had time to do it. He saw Thomas then and waved him down.

"Instead of upgrading, let's just get all new computers. We can do it, but no one wanted to mess with it. I have a name of a buddy that I trust to transfer the files over, unless you can do it." She told him she could but didn't want to do it. "You'll be fine, but if you call Gary, just tell him that he can do what he needs."

"It might be expensive. I know this place that can give you some money for the computers if you want to sell them. It's a homeless shelter on Tenth that uses older models to help people get a feel for them, and sometimes they use them for typing up resumes as well. Can I look into that?"

He grinned. "You do whatever you want with them. But you know to have them wiped, right?" She said she'd take care of it. "Also, see if you can talk Gary into giving you a nice discount and we'll donate a few newer ones, too. It's a nice thing that you're doing, and we might as well make it count for something."

By the time he'd hung up with her, he had given her permission to get a new desk for her as well as a couple of new chairs for the lobby. Not that he needed to give her permission, but she seemed to need it. Their building wasn't huge, but it was nice. He even asked her to see if his mom would help out on getting that updated, too. After he closed his phone, he realized he'd forgotten to tell her he loved her, but smiled. He'd just have to work twice as hard to show her when he got home.

He sat down and spoke to his brothers about everything that was going on. Each of them, Rider most of all, were happy that she was there as well as everything she was having done. Carter suggested that they get her some roses, and they all agreed. Before they got up to take care of business again, they had ordered six dozen roses for her that were to be delivered today. And two dozen for their mom. Misha was nearly skipping he was so happy to be going home.

~~~

Gary was working in Misha's office when the man came to the door. She'd locked up because the computers were down anyway and she wanted to be able to clean out the refrigerator as well. The man standing at the glass door not only startled her, but made her feel…well, itchy was all that came to mind.

"I'm sorry, we're closed." He nodded and pulled on the door again. He looked almost familiar to her but she wasn't sure where she'd seen him before. "You'll have to come back tomorrow."

"I'm their dad." Han stepped back from the door when he pulled on it again. "Open the door, young lady. I've as much right to be in there as you."

"I don't think so." He yanked harder on the door, and she heard someone come up behind her. She didn't have to turn to know it was Maribel. As soon as he saw her, he started pulling harder on the door.

"Open the fucking door. Maribel, you heard me, tell her to open the door. I want to see my sons." Han watched as Maribel reached for the door, and she put her hand on her.

"Don't do it." Maribel looked confused for several seconds, and that's when Han realized what he'd done. That compulsion thingy. He'd commanded her to do it, and she might have if Han hadn't stopped him.

"I don't want him here." Han nodded and pushed her behind her. The man was pissed now, and Han walked up to the door. She didn't want him to not hear her.

"You get your fucking ass away from here or so help me I will come out there and kick your ass all over the lot." He looked at her for several seconds. Then he threw back his head and laughed. Han felt her cat stir along her skin, and she let her.

"Which one do you belong to?" She didn't know what he meant, and more than likely wouldn't have answered him anyway had she understood. "You're Carter's bitch, right? That boy never could figure out what was up on a woman. He isn't going to be happy with you when he finds out you insulted his dad."

Han reached for Misha. She'd never done that before and didn't know if it would work, but he answered her right away. He was happy, and she almost told him never mind, but the man pulled on the door again.

There's a man here that says he's your father. And he's upset your mom. Please tell me that I don't have to listen to him. She felt his fear. *I'm just fine. He's on the other side of the locked door, and Gary is here if he gets stupid...well, stupider.*

Don't let him in. And call the police if he tries anything. I'm serious. I don't think he'll hurt you, but it's been twenty-five years since...just protect my mother.

I won't let anyone harm her. But I had to stop her from opening the door. He did some sort of mind thing on her. He asked her if she was affected by it. *No. All I wanted to do was hit him.*

Because you're stronger than him. She didn't know about all that, but she did want to murder the man. And all he'd done was pull on the door and upset Maribel. *We're loading up now. I'm going to take an earlier flight out so that—*

And do what? Sheesh, by the time you get here, he'll be gone. Don't come here like I need you to bring the cavalry down. I'm a big mean-assed leopard, and I can whoop his ass. She looked at the man who was still yanking on the door. *I'm fine, as is your mom. If he gives me too much more trouble, I'll just shift and tear his throat out.*

He laughed. It was tense, but he did laugh. *I'll be home in the morning. And so you know, you're going to pay for scaring me like that. I'm thinking I'll have you strip down naked and run through the woods again. I would love to take you out there again.*

Misha, this is neither the time nor the place to be getting me all hot and bothered. I have work to do, and even if I did want to do something about it, there are too many people around. She moved to the door when Mr. Lanning pounded on it. *Right now, I'm going to kick me some major ass verbally. And I have a lot of experience with that.*

I love you. She knew that she'd said it to him the other day. And as much as she wanted to say it to him now, she was afraid. *It's okay if you can't say it again. The fact that you did once is enough for now.*

I was nervous when you didn't say anything. I thought...well, I thought that you'd changed your mind. He told her he hadn't and never would. *I'm sorry but I have to go. This fool is going to piss me off.*

She felt him there, just in the back of her mind, as she approached the door. Mr. Lanning was testing her nerves today, and if he wasn't careful he was going to test her cat as well. She hit the door with her open palm and had him stepping back.

"You either go away right fucking now or so help me, I'm going to come out there and tear you a new ass. I've had it up to my eyes with you, and you've only been here twenty minutes." He opened his mouth to say something, and she cut him off. "You are walking on thin ice, asshole. Either leave now or I get the boys to come after you and show you what it's like when you fuck with one of their own."

"You think you scare me?" She nodded and smiled at him. "I want to talk to my son. Get Misha right now and I'll go away. He's my son, and I have every right to talk to him."

Maribel stood up and looked at him. In a calm and surprisingly strong voice, she spoke to her ex-husband. "You gave that right up years ago. And now that they're happy, you want to come into their lives and hurt them again? I don't think so. You stay away from here or so help me—"

He shifted. And when he lunged for the door, breaking the glass, Han did the only thing she could think to do. Her cat took her so quickly that she was on top of the man before she knew it.

He never stood a chance. Not only was her cat bigger than his, but she was pissed off, too. As she held him in her jaws, Han felt someone come up behind her. Her low growl stopped the person, but he only laughed.

"It's Gary, Hannah. I'm not going to touch you, but I'm going to make sure you're all right. Misha felt you shift and your anger." She growled again when he came closer. "Okay, I'll stay here. But if you could let up just a little on Andy's throat, I'll talk to him. Okay?"

She found she didn't want to. Not only that, but she wanted to bite down harder. The cat beneath her started to whimper, and Gary told him to shift. As soon as he did, after five more minutes of telling him he'd live longer if he did, she was holding a human and not a cat. The long scratches across his face startled her.

"You cut him when you lunged at him. They won't heal either, until he talks to your mate." Han was going to find a fucking book on this crap if it was the last thing she did. "Hannah, I'm going to talk to him. Misha said that you could talk to me, too. Do you know how?"

She didn't want to think of talking to anyone; she wanted this man to pay. Her cat bit down harder, and the man cursed at her. When she nipped harder, she got a mouth full of blood, and he stopped moving.

"She fucking bit me." Gary laughed. "I'm not having this bitch looking for me all the time. Tell her to let me go and I won't hurt her."

"You'd better be more worried about Misha. This is his mate." The man looked up at her, and she felt...no, she tasted his fear. "He's pissed, Andy. I mean, it's all I can do to keep him calm. The fact that she's taken you should tell you how strong that boy of yours is."

"I never did a thing to her. She attacked—" She bit harder, and he shut up. He glared but never said anything as she held him.

Tell him if he apologizes to Maribel and Misha, I'll think about letting him go. Gary told Andy what she'd said. *Then tell him if he wants to live for a little while longer, he'll leave this area and never return.*

"She can't tell me what to do." Gary said she was and she could. "This is just stupid. My kids should have more respect for me than this. You tell her that I'll do this, but I'm not leaving until I talk to my son."

Does he know I can hear him? Gary laughed and told her he did. *All right. I'm going to let him go, but you stand back. I don't want you to get hurt by him.*

She let him go slowly. There was no reason why he should be able to get up and hurt one of them. And as much as she wanted to tear his throat out, he was Misha's dad. When he was free, she stepped back and licked her lips. He glared at her.

"You think this is over, missy? I got news for you. My son will not take kindly to you treating his dad this way." Han licked her paws and then yawned. She loved it when he stood up and glared. She looked at his naked body and felt a little sorry for the man. He'd really let himself go.

"Misha said to tell you that he'll be here at noon tomorrow. If you're brave enough to come and face them, he suggests that you be on time. Otherwise, he said to fuck off."

When Mr. Lanning left, Han moved back into the office. Maribel was sitting at the table just staring off into space. Han put her head on her lap.

"I should have been the one to rip his throat out." Han licked her hand that had been cut by something. "It's fine, honey. I'm just glad he didn't hurt you. Misha will kick his ass."

Of that, there was little doubt.

CHAPTER 14

Misha was off the plane and down the tarmac before his brothers were even unbuckled. He had asked Gary to pick him up, but by the time he'd found the man, his brothers were right with him. He turned to them to tell him he was going to do this alone.

"Don't even say it." He cocked a brow at Andrew. "She's our sister and he fucked with her. We're going to make sure she's all right. Then you can have her. But we all felt when she was upset."

"She handled him." Rider patted him on the back, and Misha found himself wanting to hug them all. Rider must have sensed it and pulled him closer. The hug made him feel better than he had in months.

"Our Hannah is a hell of a girl." Misha nodded at Carter. "And when I see her, I'm going to kick her ass after I hug her. She scared the shit out of me."

"I didn't know…I had no idea you guys could feel her, too." Rider nodded, as did the rest of them. "She's your bitch. Do you guys…is that okay with you? I mean, I know that it doesn't matter really, but I'd like for you guys to like her."

"Are you kidding? She's fucking amazing. I can't wait until you guys have kids. I'm going to watch them become little, you guys." Misha stared at Thomas. When Thomas closed his mouth for him, they all laughed. "The way you two have sex all the time, it's only a matter of when, not if. I can't wait." Neither could Misha.

The drive over was loud due to them making fun of him. Misha had never been one that they teased, but today they seemed to be taking a great deal of enjoyment in it. As they pulled up in front of the office, he saw that a crew was already there putting in a new door, as well as two cable company vans. He moved into the door just behind Rider. And when Rider stopped suddenly, Misha bumped into him. Misha started to make fun of him but looked up, too.

"Christ." She was…she was gorgeous. She'd been beautiful before he'd left, but now…Christ, now she looked like a dream.

"They were hoping to be done before you got here." The others crowded into the room behind him, and he heard Carter laugh. Thomas gave a low wolf whistle, and Phillip made a noise in the back of his throat. "You guys are making me nervous. Is it that bad?"

"Bad? Christ, woman, are you kidding me?" He moved forward and ran his fingers down her cheek. "You are simply amazing. I want to see the whole picture. Can you stand up?"

She did, slowly, and then turned for him. The dress she had on was modest, even a little old fashioned, but she made it so sexy that he wanted to toss her onto the desk and show her how much he did indeed like it. When she faced him again, he told his brothers to go away. They laughed but left them.

"I have some messages for you." He nodded and moved forward as she backed away from him. "Some of them are really important."

"I don't really care right now." He took the slips from her and tossed them over his shoulder. Next, he bent at the waist and, putting his shoulder into her belly, picked her up. She squeaked but didn't try to get away. When he was in his office, he shut the door and locked it.

"You're going to miss the appointment I set up with you." He pulled his shirt off over his head and dropped it as he toed off his shoes. "It was with me, of course, and we were going to have a picnic dinner after we played in the woods."

"Take off your clothes." She shook her head. "If I have to strip you down, you're going home naked. I need to taste you."

"You're messing up my plans." She didn't look to him like she really cared as she kicked off her heels. "I'll have you know that I worked really hard on this for you. I was going to be sexy for you."

"You're almost too sexy for me now. Take off the blouse." She pulled it free of the tiny skirt and then unbuttoned it. She never took her eyes off him as she unzipped her skirt then let it drop to the floor. He could see her panties, but not much of them. He needed more.

"I've been shopping." He nodded, and the blouse opened slowly. "They have the most amazing underthings at this shop in the mall. I'm going to buy more of them when you pay me."

"I'll buy you the store if you show me what it is you're hiding under there." She finished the buttons, then pulled the blouse open. He could see the small triangle at her pussy and the tiniest clasp in the front of her bra. "Take it off."

"What are you going to do about your father?" He nodded. "Misha, that's not an answer. He nearly had your mom doing what he wanted. He's going to hurt her."

"He'll never hurt you or her again. I promise." Misha felt his cock ache as he watched her. But without an answer, he was afraid she might stop what she was doing. "I'm taking care of him. Maybe not today, but soon. He's gone too far."

He watched her peel the bra from her arms, then over her breasts. When she had it in her hand, just resting on her fingers, he looked at what she'd unveiled for him. He felt as if he'd been shown a great gift.

"You should see me in the yellow one." He nodded, and moved forward. "It's tinier than this one. And the cups on the bra are transparent."

"I need you to sit on my desk. I thought I could simply take you, show you how much I loved you and missed you, but right now all I can think about is being buried deep inside of you and letting go." He moved toward her, taking off his pants as he moved. His boxers were stained on the front, still wet from his cock being simply too full.

"I want you to eat me." He nearly fell over. "Lick my pussy until I come down your throat. Then I want you to fuck me that way, with your tongue and mouth on me."

"Open for me." She spread her legs and the small piece of lace hid nothing. He could see her lips now; her pussy was almost eating the silk as it soaked it. He slid his finger into her as she leaned back and then took his finger to his mouth.

"Are you going to fuck me, Misha? Bring me to climax several times while you do?" He nodded, incapable of speech. "I need to feel you inside of me. Either your tongue or your cock, but I need you to fill me."

Misha dropped to his knees before her and lifted her ass up to bring her closer to the edge of his desk. He buried his face in her heat and inhaled deeply. She cried out when he slid his finger into her tight hole.

"I'm going to come." He held her while she flooded his mouth. Misha drank as much as he could, but he knew that he'd missed more than he'd gotten. When she told him she was coming again, he slid his other finger into her pussy and fucked her hard. She came screaming his name.

Standing up, he freed his cock. She was panting, and he wanted to pound into her until he couldn't move. When she reached for him, he laved her nipple with his tongue and bit into her creamy breast. Hannah held him to her as she fisted his cock. Misha was so close to the edge that he had to put his hand over hers.

"I can't. You have to let me inside." She nodded and leaned back again. It was a feast. It was all he could think of. When she cupped her breasts and tugged at her nipples, he pulled his boxers down and off as he stepped between her legs. She wrapped her ankles around him and pulled him closer.

"Fuck me." He nodded but only entered her with his crown. "Please, Misha. More. I need more."

"Say it. I want to hear you say it again." She nodded but said nothing. "Tell me, Hannah, and I'll give you what we both want."

"I love you." He filled her. She cried out and he nearly joined her when her sheath rippled along his cock, strangling it so tightly that he ached with it, but he waited. When she looked up at him, Misha kissed her gently on the mouth as he held her to him.

"I love you. I love you with all my heart." He kissed her again. "I want to marry you as soon as possible. I want you big with our child."

Her scream had him releasing. As soon as she dug her nails into his back and her teeth into his shoulder, Misha came again, filling her with his seed, and still he needed more. Pulling free of her, he pulled her off the desk and flipped her around. She seemed to understand and bent at the waist and held on. Misha took her hard, holding her hips still for him as he fucked her hard enough to move the desk a good foot. When he came this time, he threw back his head and howled, something he'd never done in his life during sex.

~~~

The knock at the door startled her, and she looked at Misha. He'd been holding her on his lap for the last five minutes after they'd dressed—she'd had to put on one of his shirts again— and she didn't want to be bothered. He called out the door for the person to go away.

"I'd love to, but you have a visitor. It's Bella." Han felt the hair on her arms dance, and she stiffened. But Misha simply said to let her in. Before Han could tell him no, the door was opening and her mother was suddenly there.

"You gots my daughter and I want her back right now. I don't know what you thinks it is you're doing, but she's mine and I need her to come back and care for me." Misha asked her to sit down. "I don't want to be social with you. I want you to tell me where my daughter is."

"I'm right here." Her mother stared at her for several seconds before she took the chair Misha had offered her. "What did you think I'd do, Mother, simply forget that you nearly killed me and come running back home to you?"

"I didn't hurt you no more'n you hurt me. You should have seen her hitting on me that morning. It was all I could do to save myself." Misha laughed, and Han felt her stomach turn. "I have never raised a hand to her first. It was all I could do to save my face sometimes. I was the victim in all this here stuff. She was forever hitting on me first. You know that."

"You mean like you did to her birth mother?" Han was looking at her mother when she paled, and knew that whatever Misha knew, her mother knew as well. "The injuries that she sustained were not something that she would have had from the accident. She'd been beaten. With a bat, they think."

"You don't know what you're talking about. She's my daughter. I had her." Misha shook his head and stood up, putting Han in his chair. "You just give her back to me and we'll call it even. I won't even ask you for the money I was gonna."

"You're not going to get either, so that's good." Han watched as Rider and Thomas came into the room. This time the door was left open. "You should also know that you're a prime suspect in the death of one Shadow Dark, also known as Peter Dark."

"I don't know nobody by that name. What the hell are you on? I didn't kill nobody." Her mother looked at the other two men. "What you going to do? Have them hold me while you fuck me? I gots news for you. They won't have to hold me long. I've been wanting a piece of you for some time."

When she started to stand again, Rider pushed her back into the chair and told her to shut up. Thomas came to the other side of the table where Han was and handed her a thick file. He winked at her before he turned to her mother.

"Dark was the man you bludgeoned to death when you were at the hospital a few weeks ago. We have surveillance video that shows you getting into the car with him, giving him head, and then killing him." Han knew the moment Bella realized who he was talking about. "But what we're really here about is Hannah's mother. You killed her to take the baby."

"I don't know what you're talking about. And even if I did take that baby she birthed, you gots no proof that I did a thing." Thomas handed Han and Bella each a picture of the woman Han had always thought of as her mother with a tiny little bundle in her arms. "Where did you get this?"

"The bus station. Right after you killed Kelli Little."

Han stared at the picture. It wasn't the woman who she had always thought of as her mother that had her attention. It was the bundle she held in her hands. The blanket that was wrapped around her was stained. Even though it was a black and white photo, Han knew it was blood. Her real mother's blood.

"You killed her?" Her mother...Bella stared at her and smiled. "You actually killed her to take me? Why?"

"Why do you think? I can't have me no kids and the welfare office was giving away money like it was free to people who had a bunch of brats." She laughed then, high and manic. "Course it was free, but I needed a little more. And there she was, straining to bring you into the world."

"I don't understand you." Bella laughed again and winked at Misha. He said nothing but sat on the corner of his desk. "You killed her for more welfare money?"

"I helped her birth you." She said it like that should have justified it all. "I mean, I had to do something, she was hurting real bad. So I gave her a little of what I had on me and she was ever so grateful that she gave you to me.

That's what I'm going to tell anybodies that asks me anyway."

"But that's not what happened, is it?" Bella laughed as she sat back in the chair. Misha asked her again.

"I tell you whatever you want me to if you give me a bit of whatever you give her. I'm just as pretty as she is, but I gots me some experience she'll never have." Han felt her skin crawl and her cat push at her to kill. Misha took her hand but said nothing. She held onto him like a lifeline.

Thomas cleared his throat and nodded to Rider, who went to the door again. This time when Thomas spoke, it was to the police that were just behind Bella. Han knew this had been set up.

"Tell us what happened. Han deserves to know, don't you think? She should know just where it is she came from. And when you're done, I'll make sure that you get something for your trouble." Bella adjusted herself in the chair as she smiled. "But it has to be the truth, Bella. No more lies or half-truths."

"No half-truths and you're going to pay me?" Thomas said nothing, but Bella must have taken that for a yes, because she started talking like it was something she needed to get off her chest. "I was walking down the road looking for a fix. I had me a little, but I knew that it wasn't going to last me long. Anyways, I see this wreck. A van was overturned and they was bodies spilling out into the street. I thought there'd be something there. I got in as close as I could and that's when I spied her. She'd made her way to the other side of the road and I go and sit with her."

"She was in labor?" Bella nodded and smiled at Thomas. "You have to tell me the truth or it won't go well."

"She was. Real close to the end, too. Her head had a bump on it about here." Bella pointed to the middle of her forehead. "But it wasn't bleeding all that much. She was straining hard, and when she asked me to find her somebody to take her into the hospital, I go over and steal her a blanket. She didn't take all that long, but before I know it, she was screaming in pain. I had to shut her up."

"Did you have intentions of killing her before you took the baby?" Bella looked at Thomas like she had no idea what he meant. "Did you want the baby or did you want to kill Kelli?"

"I already told you. I wanted the kid, but not really. This was just a spur of the minute kind of thing. But then once she told me how her mommy and daddy didn't want her anymore, I knew that nobody would miss her, or the brat. I wasn't going to have her coming around telling them welfare people how the brat was hers, now could I? That would have messed things up for me."

"Of course." Misha stood up and pulled Han into his arms as he glared at Bella. "Just finish the story please."

"Well, after I helped her, she started crying. Begging me for a phone to show her mommy and daddy what a pretty baby she'd had. I told her I din't have no phone but told her I could take the baby off her hands for her and she'd be able to go back to their house." Bella laughed. "It was all she wrote. I had to shut her up real quick like, so I hit her in the head. Then when she tried to crawl away, holding on to my baby, I hit her again and again. There wasn't a soul around to hear her then."

Her laughter made Han turn to her. "You killed her for me and then you treated me like I was nothing more than a housemaid for you."

"So? That's all I wanted you for anyway. That and the extra money, of course. You know how much more they give you when you gots a brat? Lots, let me tell you." Bella stood up. "Now that you have what you wanted, I'll just take Han with me and that money you promised me."

"I didn't promise you money." Bella lunged for Thomas but was stopped by the police. "All I said was you would get something. The police asked us to see what we could get from you, and you surprised me by giving it all to us. Including the murder of Dark."

"You lied to me. Damn it all to hell. Ain't there nobody nice in the world anymore?" She turned to the police and smiled at them. "You let me go and I'll make it worth your while. I gots me some ideas on how to please a man that will make your pecker beg."

Han sat down in Misha's chair. She felt numb. More than that she felt…nothing. When she looked up, all six of the Lanning men were in the room with her, as well as Maribel. She looked over at Misha.

"How long have you known?" He told her only since they'd left. "And you never thought to warn me that she wasn't my mother and that she'd come here?"

"No. I mean yes. I was going to tell you when I got here, but you distracted me." She flushed, and he stood up. Han stopped him from coming toward her by raising her hand. "I wanted to tell you in person. I didn't think…no, I wanted to hold you while we told you what we thought. It wasn't until we got here that we knew not only that she'd done it for sure, but we also knew who your birth mother was. Thomas heard from her family as we drove here."

"They know about me?" Thomas nodded. "And what do they think? That they want me to stay away from them? I have no desire to bother them."

"No. They want to meet you. They had…when Kelli left home, she was on her way to college. They had no idea that she was pregnant until a month after she'd left. At first they were upset, mad even, but they never stopped loving her. In fact, they've been trying to find her. The accident report had never mentioned her or you, so they didn't think to look there. Kelli had changed her name so she wouldn't embarrass them."

Han didn't say anything more, and Thomas laid a picture in front of her. She stared at the picture. There was little doubt this was her mother. They looked like they could be twins. She ran her finger down her cheek and then looked up at Misha.

"She killed her for no other reason than to have more welfare. She never wanted me, never loved me. She only wanted me so that she could…so she could hurt me." Misha held her as she sobbed. Han felt her heart shatter with every breath she took. Her mother was dead and her entire life had been a lie.

Misha held her until she stopped crying. Then he picked her up and held her in his arms. She'd never been loved until now. Had never had anyone care for her even just a little. Closing her eyes, she thought of all that she'd missed and decided that she wasn't going to miss anything else.

"I love you, Misha Lanning. And if this hasn't made you change your mind, I will marry you." He kissed her head and told her tomorrow. Han fell asleep knowing that he'd protect her forever.

CHAPTER 15

Maribel watched them as they sat around the table. She had never thought that her sons would come to love one little woman as much as they did Hannah. And from the looks of it, she loved them just as much. When Misha stood up, the room grew quiet, and Maribel held her breath.

"As you guys know, this is my mate. What you might not know is that she loves me." The room burst out in laughter. "I know, shocked me, too."

"You don't love him as much as you do me, do you, Hannah?" Rider put his hand over his heart as he continued. "Please tell me that you're going to dump him and spend your days loving me."

"I'd kill you the first time we went to bed together." Again, the laughter rang around the table. Hannah stood up next to Misha as she looked around the room. "I have come to love you all. Some less than others, Rider, but I do love you."

The others got up and patted Misha on the back, then hugged Hannah. When she sat down again, the boys sat as well. Maribel couldn't have been happier. But Misha cleared his throat.

"Hannah has said that she thinks that you should know what happened the day I was shot. She knows that you're worried and have fears that I'll get hurt again. And to be truthful about it, if I had to do it over again, I'd do it the same way." He looked at Rider. "I didn't want you to die."

Rider stood up and hugged Misha to him. They hugged several more times before Rider sat down. She could feel the emotion between them, and when Misha started talking, Rider took her hand.

"He knew that if he killed them that we'd be called in. It was his plan all along to have the Lanning team come to his place and find him. He'd been planning this for years. Since his sister had died." Rider nodded. "I knew that you'd figured it out, but I didn't want to say anything in the off chance that you hadn't. I should have come clean as soon as I woke up."

"I had dated his sister in high school. Mel Donaldson. She'd been so sweet on me that it was the only reason that...I didn't want her to be hurt, so when we went out, I told her that I would date her but it would never be anything more." Rider looked down instead of at his family. "She said she understood. We decided that we'd go with each other to the rest of the dances that year and then from there we'd see. But at some point, she fell in love with me. And as hard as I tried, I couldn't get her to understand that I didn't love her. She told me she'd told her brother the day she killed herself."

"Oh, that poor girl. And you. I'm so sorry, Rider." Maribel didn't think she could have loved Hannah more, but she did at that moment when she hugged Rider to her again. "You must have been devastated."

"I didn't know what to think. I had...the police asked me what had happened so many times that day that I felt as if I'd done it instead of her hanging herself. And when her parents came to the station with the note, I was released."

Misha nodded at him, and Maribel watched her second oldest son. "She had said that I never loved her, but it wasn't my fault. That we'd had an arrangement and her falling in love with me wasn't part of the deal. She'd even told them that I had tried, several times as a matter of fact, to make sure she knew we were just friends, but she couldn't live without me. She hung herself at the park where we'd played ball the day before."

"Her brother couldn't live with that. He said that he was going to kill you, and it was...." Misha looked at Hannah as he continued. "I shoved you out of the way when the first shot was fired. I was terrified that after he killed me that he'd go after you. He knew what we were, you know. He had it all planned out. Bob told me that he was going to enjoy this more than anything he'd ever done before." Maribel closed her eyes and let Misha weave the scene for her.

The three of them were in the big empty building. The stench of blood was everywhere, but Bob didn't care how the people died so long as it brought the Lannings to him. When they found the den he'd been in, Rider had gone in just ahead of Misha, and it was then that he heard the bullet being racked into the chamber.

Misha threw Rider out of the way. He'd hit his head, but he could still hear his heart beating. When Bob had moved toward him, to fire at him again, Misha attacked. That's when he was shot the first time. His chest, he said, exploded in pain. Then, when the gun jammed, Misha had attacked, knowing that if he didn't, if he were to die now, that Rider would be dead, too. Instead of giving in, he ran at him and got shot a second time.

"By the time I was too weak to fight much more, I had managed to snap his neck. I don't know how I managed it, but thankfully I did." Misha sat down and pulled Hannah into his lap as he continued. "I didn't tell you…I couldn't tell you before because I didn't want you to feel like it was your fault that I'd been shot. I needed for you to think this was just another murderer who had gotten the better of me."

"But you knew." Hannah nodded when Rider spoke to her. "How? No one knew about me finding out but me. I never told a soul."

"You told Billy." She turned on Misha's lap and looked at him. "I didn't know you then. None of you but Billy did. One night when my…when Bella had beaten me up, he told me the story you'd told him, the one where the girl had loved you. He told me but never your names. I think he was only doing it because he needed someone to tell. He never meant to misplace your trust. It wasn't until Misha told me how he got the small scar that I knew it was you. I hope you won't be mad at Billy."

"Never."

After they settled down into teasing each other again, Maribel looked around at her sons. Soon they wouldn't need her any longer. They'd all have their own families and mates. She felt her heart break a little for herself.

She looked up when Hannah, as they had all started calling her, sat beside her. The child was just simply the most beautiful thing she'd ever seen, and her heart was filled with only goodness. As they sat there listening to the men banter back and forth, Maribel thought of the children she'd have and was excited for it. When Hannah turned to her, Maribel knew that she'd love this child like her own forever.

"I want you to move in with Misha and me." Maribel was startled and not sure what to say. But Hannah continued before she could make a fool of herself. "I've talked to him about it. He is…Misha is all for it. In fact, he's more than for it. He's very excited."

"Whatever would I do in that big house? Besides, I have this one." She nodded and smiled. "You're up to something. And here I was thinking how much I'd fallen in love with you."

"Thomas wants to live in your house. With the others. But Misha and I, well, we want you close to us. I want you close to me." She looked away then, and Maribel held her breath. "I've never had a real mother. And now I find out, I didn't even have the one I had. I need you to come and show me how to…I need you to love me and show me what it's like to be a mom. I would very much like it if I could call you 'Mom.'"

"You want to call me 'Mom?'" Hannah said yes but only if it was okay. "Okay? Good Lord, child, it would be wonderful. As for living with you and Misha, I will only do it on one condition."

"Anything." Maribel nodded and didn't say anything. The possibilities were endless, but she truly only wanted one thing. "You'll do it?"

"Don't you want to know what it is I want?" Hannah smiled and shook her head. "It might be more than you're willing to give."

"Not possible. I have all I want right here, and you'd never take that from me. If you want it, I'll do my very best to give it to you. Even a grandchild." Maribel felt her eyes fill. "That's it, isn't it? You want a grandchild?"

"I do. I do more than anything in this world." Hannah reached for her hand and squeezed it. Then they sat there for a little while longer. She had no idea what moving in with her son would take and right now, didn't care in the least. She was going to be a grandma soon.

~~~

Hannah was sitting at the kitchen table when he came down the stairs the next morning. He'd hoped that he would wake her by making her scream out another climax, but her side of the bed was cold, and no matter how many times he tried to reach her, she was blocking him. Misha looked at Jackson when he cleared his throat.

"She had a phone call. I'm not sure who it was, but she's been sitting there since she hung up. I've fed her breakfast and given her some tea, but she hasn't said a word." Jackson handed him a cup of tea. "See if you can get her to drink a little more. I worry about the young mistress."

Misha sat down and lifted up her chin so that she had to look at him. Hannah stared at him for several seconds before she finally smiled. It wasn't really that reassuring, however. It was as sad as he'd ever seen her face.

"They called." He frowned. "My...whatever. The people who are my grandparents. They called here this morning. The lawyer that you told me to talk to, he transferred them to this phone but didn't give them the number."

Misha nodded. "And what did your grandparents say to you? I take it that they want to meet you."

"Yes. Well, no. I'm not really sure. They do want to meet me, but on their terms. They want...I don't want to go there. I'm not going to...I don't think this will work out." He asked her why not. "Because they want me to come and live with them for a while. They want...Christ, I don't know. They want me to be a part of their family now, and living with them is their only option. Why?"

"I don't know." He looked at Jackson when he pushed the cup of tea at them. "Did they sound like they were pissed because you won't do it? Or did you tell them that you weren't yet?"

"I told them I was happy right here and that I'm not really thrilled about moving in with them. I don't know where that is now. The man, his name is Howard Little, said that he'd like to meet you, too. I'm not...I don't want them in my life."

Misha nodded. He wasn't sure what to tell her and looked up when his mom walked in the room. He told her what was going on.

"Well, of course he wants you to live with him. He more than likely kicked his daughter out when she was pregnant and now feels guilty for it. You're his only connection to her, and he wants to make up for it." His mom sat down and took Hannah's hand. "You do what you want. We'll be your family, and if they want to come here, we'll make them welcome. If they piss you off, just shift and eat them. Now, can I have a cup of that wonderful tea, Jackson? And one of those scones if you have them handy?"

Misha stared at his mom. Christ, the older she got the more her filter seemed to be disappearing. But when Hannah giggled, then laughed out loud, Misha smiled as well. She was wiping at tears the longer she sat there. Soon, she got up and hugged his mom.

"I think I shall refer them to you when they call here again. Mrs. Little sounds like a doormat, and the mister sounded like he was used to getting his way. Not that I'm not used to that sort of temperament, but I've decided that I like me just like I am right now and I'm not changing to suit him." Hannah kissed his mom. "Thank you. I feel better about this already."

The plan for the day was to move the rest of his mom's things into the house. Thomas was the only one that expressed a desire to stay at her house, as the others had opted to move into apartments or buy. Only Rider had decided to build his own home. Misha thought it was a control thing, but he insisted that it was because he wanted the counters at the right height.

Looking at the counters in his kitchen, all he could think about was sitting Hannah on them and taking her right now. He stood up and asked her if she'd join him in the office. He wanted to talk to her anyway. She told him she'd be there soon. As soon as he walked into his office, he was startled out of his lusty musings when the phone rang.

"My name is Daniel with the Colorado state police. Is this Mr. Misha Lanning?" He told him it was and pulled a notebook toward him to take notes. "I'm...I'm not really sure where to begin. As I said, my name is Daniel Little. My parents are Howard and Carole Little. I understand that you're marrying my niece, Hannah."

"I am. I understand that your parents talked to Hannah this morning. She was upset about it." Daniel mumbled something, but he wasn't clear enough to understand. "I'm sorry, what did you say?"

"I hate to say this about my own parents. I love them to death, but...well, if she never comes here, she'd be better off." He let out a long sigh. "They kicked my sister out when she was just barely eighteen. She'd been gone for nearly...I guess a month before they told me what they'd done. Kelli was younger than me by almost five years, and

I was away at college when it happened. I tried for years to find her and never found anything."

"We only just caught her murderer." Daniel didn't say anything, and Misha took that as sorrow. He continued when he didn't say anything else. "Are you coming to meet Hannah?"

"I don't know." That surprised him. Misha started to speak, but Daniel did first. "She's my niece, I know, but…well, I don't know her. I'm not even sure where to begin to know her. And if my parents found out? Well, I think…you know what? Fuck it. When can I come out?"

"How about next weekend?" Daniel asked what was going on then. "I'm marrying your niece. And since you took the time to warn her about her grandparents, I'd very much like to meet you as well. I'll send a plane for you."

"I see." Daniel laughed. "She's marrying well, I take it. Doesn't matter, but my dad will not care for it. He has money as well, a great deal of it, but you'll never meet a broker man in your life. I'm going to be there. And if you'd send a plane for my wife and me, we'll enjoy that as well. Thank you."

After making arrangements for where to pick him up, Misha leaned back in his chair, only to hop up again. Hannah was taking entirely too long and he was going to find her. Maybe he'd chase her around the woods for a while before he took her to the ground. Smiling, he thought of Daniel, too.

If the man proved to be a pain in the ass, he'd simply chew him up and spit his ass out. Literally.

About the Author

Kathi Barton, author of the bestselling series Force of Nature, lives in Nashport, Ohio with her husband Paul. In addition to writing full time Kathi likes to spend time with her eight grandkids, three children and three children-in-laws. She writes to relax and have fun.

Her muse, a cross between Jimmy Stewart and Hugh Jackman brings them to life for her readers in a way that has them coming back time and again for more. Her favorite genre is paranormal romance with a great deal of spice. You can visit Kathi on line and drop her an email if you'd like. She loves hearing from her fans. aaronskiss@gmail.com.

Follow Kathi on her blog:
http://kathisbartonauthor.blogspot.com/

www.ingramcontent.com/pod-product-compliance
Lightning Source LLC
Chambersburg PA
CBHW032129170626
46808CB00006B/2158